ILLUSTRATIONS.

ILLUSTRATIONS.

TALKS BY QUEER FOLKS.

A CRY FROM A MENAGERIE.

"I CAN LAUGH."

I WISH that people now believed as many stories about hyenas as were believed in old times, for then I do not think we should be shut up in cages. People used to say that hyenas could imitate men's voices, and could call people by name. It is true that I have a very queer voice, but I do not think it is so much like a man's. People used to say, too, that hyenas could change the color of their hair whenever they wished to do so, and that in a hyena's eye was a stone that would make a man able to prophesy, if the stone were taken out and put under the man's tongue. I wonder if any of my relatives were ever killed by any man who wanted to find the stone and become a prophet?

Other folks believed that the shadow of a hyena would keep a dog from barking, and in Abyssinia hyenas used to be called "enchanters," and the people would not use the skin of a hyena till it had been prayed over by a priest.

Well, I cannot help myself, I suppose. People around here will not believe such stories, and perhaps I should be shut up, any way, if they were believed. Neighbor Coyote in the next cage says he cannot help himself, either. He told me a story that he says some of the Navajo Indians tell about him. These Indians say that the Coyote is responsible for the way the stars look in the sky. Once, say the Indians, before there were any stars in the sky at all, the old men of the Navajoes piled up a heap of stars, and gathered around the heap, ready for work. The old men had decided that they would embroider the sky the day was over, and so the Coyote traveled in a circle, and came back at night to the place where he had started in the morning.

Of course the Coyote was not to be beaten that way, so the next day he started again for the sun. But, sad to relate, the second time Coyote traveled in a circle, and came back to his starting-point.

So, the third day, he was advised by some one to go early in the morning to the eastern edge of the earth, and wait there till the sun came up.

Coyote started. He went to the eastern edge of the earth; and then, the Indians say, he sat down on the hole where the sun came up.

By and by, along came the sun up the hole, and told Coyote to get out of the way.

But Coyote did not mind. He sat there till his shoulders began to be so warm that he spat on his paws and began rubbing his back.

Then that impertinent Coyote said to the sun, "Why do you come up here meddling with me?"

But the sun said, "I am not meddling with you. I am traveling where I have a right to travel."

Then the Coyote was very impolite, and told the sun to go around some other way. But of course the sun would not do that, for the road belonged to him.

So, at last, the Coyote asked if he might go up with the sun, and the sun was so good-natured that he took him along. The Indians say that by and by the sun and the Coyote came to a path with steps — a sort of ladder; and when they both came above the world the Coyote was so hot that he did wish he could jump down. But it was so very far to the earth that he did not dare to do it.

At noon the sun was so bright that he told Coyote to shut his eyes. Coyote obeyed, but all that afternoon he kept opening and shutting his eyes, to see how near the earth was coming. And when the sun came to the west part of the world, the Coyote caught hold of the nearest tree, and came down to the ground.

But however much the Coyote in the next cage may believe this story, I do not believe it. He need not boast much before me of the Coyote that took a ride on the sun. I should not think it much honor to have had an ancestor that said to the sun, " Why do you come up here meddling with me?" and to have had the sun answer, "I am not meddling with you.   I am traveling where I have a right to travel."

Seems to me, if that were true, it would show that the old Coyote did not have very good manners.

This Coyote neighbor of mine says that there is another sun story that the Indians tell about that former Coyote. In the first place, say the Shasta Indians, the sun had nine brothers, all flaming hot like himself.   Ten suns in all!   This world was so hot that people were likely to die, but the Coyote saved them, for he went to the nine brothers and killed them all.   There was only our own present sun left.

There was great trouble, too, about the moon. The moon had nine brothers, and all were made of the coldest ice, so that at night people nearly froze. But the good Coyote took a tremendous knife of flint stone, went to the eastern edge of the world, heated stones to keep his hands warm, and there killed the nine extra moons, so that people were warm again.

Well, that Coyote neighbor of mine may boast all he pleases of these stories, yet he cannot deny that all hen-keepers hate his folks, in the country where they run wild.

Another story that has been told about us Hyenas is, that we have only one bone apiece in our necks. A great man named Aristotle once said that this was so, but I know that he was mistaken, for how could I turn my head, if my neck were one jointless bone? There was believed to be a very mysterious power in this neck-bone of the Hyena, and even now it is said that the Arabs, whenever they kill a Hyena, hide its head by burying it somewhere, for fear that the head should avenge the death of the animal.

But there is one thing that I can really do. I can laugh. It is a rather queer laugh, I suppose, but it is a better laugh than most animals can make. If you are around here when the keeper gives me my dinner, you will hear me laugh over it. I am a great deal smarter than that old fellow hanging on that tree. He is a Sloth, and I do think that he is the most stupid creature that I ever saw. He hardly stirs, but just hangs there. I should think that he would want to come down to the ground sometimes, but he never seems to, and I have heard of a farmer in South America who told a traveler that a family of black Tardos, or Sloths, had lived in a clump of

shade-trees behind the farmhouse for eleven years, and in all that time the creatures had never been seen on the ground. A Sloth would pass weeks on the same branch.

THE SLOTH THAT HUNG ON THE TREE.

Sloths do come down to the ground sometimes, however, for another traveler in South America once saw a Sloth swimming across a river. I think that Sloths must be very stupid, though, usually, for I heard of a hotel-keeper who owned a Sloth for six years, but although the same person fed him every, day, yet that Sloth never seemed to know his feeder from any other person.

And then I thought to myself that perhaps, after my poor neighbor was buried, that terrible Mrs. Ammophila might come back after me. The thought filled me with horror. I tumbled to the ground, and curled up in a little hole under the fence.

"I'll stay here and hide," I said. "O, poor, poor Mrs. Smooth-skin! To be buried that way!"

I peeped out of my crack. Part of Neighbor Smooth-skin's body still stood out above the ground, but Mrs. Ammophila struggled up and came in sight once more. She pushed the body in, and rushed at bits of earth, and poked them into the hole. She hauled on dirt. Alas! alas! Neighbor Smooth-skin was entirely buried. I should never see her again. Mrs. Ammophila had covered her completely.

"Well, if there is any more burying to be done, there will have to be another hole dug first," I thought. "I'll crawl away while she's digging. Oh! if Neighbor Smooth-skin had only known enough to crawl away beforehand."

But, that minute, Mrs. Ammophila suddenly flew away.

I waited. She did not come back.

"She didn't want me because I am hairy," I concluded. "My long tufts of hair would have partly protected me from the stab. Mrs. Ammophila could not have given it with certainty, as she could to a smooth-skinned caterpillar; and if I were not stabbed, you had better believe I would wriggle so that Mrs. Ammophila would have a very hard time carrying me to the tomb."

I knew why she had buried my neighbor. You see, I had heard stories of such things before, but I had not recognized Mrs. Ammophila as being one of the murderers, that is all. Such creatures as she bury other insects, putting an egg by them so that, when the egg is hatched, the little grub that comes from it may find something to eat. Mrs. Ammophila's grub will feed on my poor Neighbor Smooth-skin, who honestly intended to become a moth.

Mrs. Ammophila tries to be very fine now, going around daintily sipping the juice of pink or blue flowers, but she must have spent her childhood underground in a hole, eating a poor, paralyzed caterpillar.

I suppose she might not like to have such a fact referred to now, but it is true, any way.

I know of a good many other murders that have been committed in this yard. There are some creatures here called Oxybelus that pounce on flies and bury them in holes in the ground, the way poor Neighbor Smooth-skin was buried. Why, sometimes one of those fly-killers will bury as many as seven flies in one hole! The flies are light enough, so that Mrs. Fly-killer can carry them through the air, one at a time. Mrs. Fly-killer will come sailing along, holding a poor fly that seems as quiet as if it were dead, and will plunge into the somewhat sandy place where she has dug her burrow, leave the fly below ground, and let her hole stay covered up every time she goes off after another fly. I suppose she is afraid to leave the burrow open, for fear something should go in there while she is away. Mrs. Fly-killer is about the size of a fly herself, and is black. She has to carry the fly by her hind feet, because she has to use her fore ones in opening her burrow. She is very lively, and hops around a good deal. I should think she was nervous.

There is another little creature that comes around here and catches spiders, and buries them in holes in the ground.   I saw one of these spider-killers dragging a red jumping-spider over the ground the other day. The spider-killer was hurrying him toward a little hole she had dug.   The spider was perfectly quiet, and let her do anything she pleased with him.   He had been stabbed, I suppose, and was to furnish a living for one of Mrs. Spider-killer's children.   That poor spider lies buried by that leaf at the foot of that weed.   You never would know by the looks of the ground that anything was underneath.   The spider-killer did not fly with the red spider.   She only hauled him along as fast as she could.   I have heard that there is an old saying:

> " If you wish to live and thrive,
> Let a spider run alive."

But Mrs. Spider-killer does not care anything about old sayings.   Her business in life is to make war with spiders, and see that they go underground properly. She must be more brave than Mrs. Fly-killer or Mrs. Caterpillar-killer, for neither the flies nor the caterpillars can do any harm to their murderers; but if the spider should bite Mrs. Spider-killer in the contest, I am afraid she would come to grief, instead of the spider she meant to bury.

I do not know whether the spider-killers of this yard ever pounce on spiders that are in their webs, but I have heard that there is in France an insect called Pelopæus, that dares do so. It does not seem afraid, but rather enjoys the fight. The Pelopæus has a very strong sting, and if that once touches the spider the poor fellow is doomed. Folks say that the Pelopæus is very prudent, and flies so carefully about the web that the spider is stung before he can do anything. But if the spider is ready, sometimes the Pelopæus feels some threads thrown around her, and the spider winds her up and kills her. This seldom happens, though. That Pelopæus will manage to carry two or three spiders to her nest, sometimes.

You may wonder how I know all this, but that spider up in the apple-tree told me about it. That spider says she is not going to be buried, if she can help it.

"That Pelopæus in France does not bury spiders in the ground," said she; "she puts them into a nest of clay and then seals the nest. But no spider-killer is going to catch me. I'm going to keep wide awake. Do you suppose I want to be paralyzed, and poked into a hole and kept for food for Mrs. Spider-killer's child? Indeed, I don't! Why, do you know, down in Texas there is a kind of insect called the Tarantula-killer, because it carries off and buries the big spider that is called the "tarantula," but is not one really. That great spider is buried several inches underground. It's dreadful the way that Pompilus does."

"That what?" I questioned.

"Pompilus," said the apple-tree spider. "The Tarantula-killer's real name is *Pompilus formosus*. It's most as long a name as my spider-web, isn't it? There are other insects that have Pompilus for a name, too. There is one called *Pompilus tropicus*, that wears a red band. What do you suppose 'Pompilus' means?"

"I don't know, I'm sure," I answered.

It always makes me feel very ignorant when I hear

that apple-tree spider talking. She knows so much more than I know. And she talks so easily, too.

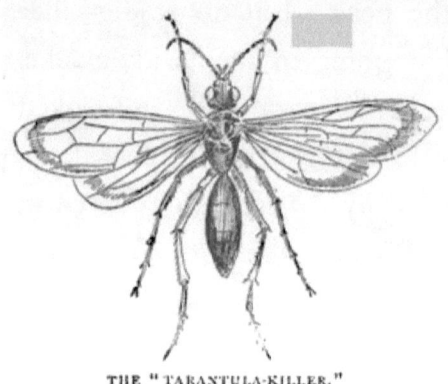

THE "TARANTULA-KILLER."

"Pompilus is a name that comes from a word meaning an 'escort,'" explained the apple-tree spider, "but I don't want any such escort to the grave as that. Do you?"

"O, no, no, indeed!" I cried. "Poor Neighbor Smooth-skin! I am so sorry such a thing happened to her! Were any of your neighbors or relatives ever buried that way?"

"Plenty of them," responded the apple-tree spider grimly; "plenty of them. Why, the spider-killers got

POMPILUS TROPICUS.

my mother, two of my cousins, my aunt, and my — Whew! There is one of those spider-killers now!"

The apple-tree spider hid under a piece of bark, and our conversation was at an end; but I mean to be just as careful as she is, and keep away from Mrs. Ammophila and all her tribe. We caterpillars and flies and spiders need to exercise a great deal of caution in this back yard, or we shall come to a dreadful end, some of us.

You see, besides the enemies that want to bury us, there are some that want to kill us another way. They are the Ichneumon folks. They will come along and stab one, putting an egg either outside or inside a caterpillar, and that caterpillar, instead of being dragged off to be buried, will go on living and crawling

ICHNEUMON SUTURALIS.

about; but the ichneumon's egg will hatch, and the grub will be eating the caterpillar all the time, and when the caterpillar is exhausted it dies, and the new ichneumon comes out all right. That is about as bad as being buried, I think, because perhaps the buried caterpillar, being paralyzed, does not feel Mrs. Ammophila's grub eating, but I am afraid the caterpillar that is not buried does feel Mrs. Ichneumon's grub, perhaps. Any way I do not want to try the experiment. Why, there is one kind of ichneumon that is so small that its grub can live inside a plant-louse, or

APHIDIUS TRITICAPHIS.

Aphis. Sometimes I see a dead Aphis all puffed out and turned black, and I know what is the matter. The little ichneumon is inside. Its name is Aphidius, and it has killed the Aphis. I don't want any creature living inside me. I do want to live till I turn into a moth and have wings. Wings! Won't that be fine! I am going to eat as fast as I can, so as to grow as quickly as possible. That will be hurrying toward being a moth.

A BLUE-JAY'S JABBERINGS.

QUEE! Did you hear me scolding just now?
We blue-jays scold a great deal, you know, any way,
for somehow there is always enough to scold about if
one only gets into the habit of it. But the thing that
I have been scolding about now is something new.
The Buddhists, I have just heard, have been telling
something about us blue-jays — something that is not
true. I should like to know how long such a story
has been going around. A great many years, I dare
say. Men do not know very much about us birds.
The Buddhists say this: "There are four kinds of
beings who fear when there is no danger," and among
the four they mention "the bird kiralá, or the blue-jay,
that hatches its eggs with its feet upward, that, if the
sky should fall, it may be ready to support it."

Now, did you ever hear such nonsense as that about a bird? Do you suppose that I am so silly as to hatch my eggs with my feet upward? I am not a bit more afraid that the sky will fall than you are, and I should like to tell those ridiculous Buddhists that they had better find some blue-jays and observe their habits, before telling any more such stories as that. Do you wonder that I scold?

However, I have company in my affliction, for the

Buddhists go on to say that another of the "beings who fear when there is no danger" is the bird "kos likiniyá, the curlew, that treads with all gentleness lest it should shake the earth."

Now I am not very well acquainted with

THE CURLEW.

Mr. Curlew, but I am going to ask him, the very next time I see him, if that is not a story, too. I am sure he is not afraid of shaking the earth. The only thing that he is afraid of is, that he will not find worms and mollusks enough for his dinner.

If people could understand all that we birds say, folks might not be very much pleased with our remarks, always. The Jewish rabbis used to say that Solomon could understand all that the birds sang, and he would amuse himself with listening to the wise remarks that were made in bird-language. And this is what the rabbis said that Solomon heard the peacock say: "With what measure thou judgest others, thou shalt thyself be judged." What they said the raven croaked was, "The farther from man the happier I."

But I do not believe that Solomon ever knew bird-talk, and I am sure that I have heard the peacock and the raven say much more silly things than those.

In Scotland, some of the people pretend to know what a bird called the Black-throated Diver says. The people say the bird's words are, "Deoch! deoch! deoch! tha'n loch a traoghadh!" which means in your language, "Drink! drink! drink! the lake is nearly dried up!"

The relative of the Black-throated Diver, called the Red-throated Diver, has a very strange, loud cry,

THE BLACK-THROATED DIVER.

which sounds like a drowning person screaming for help, and it is very startling to people who are out on the water just about dark, to hear such a cry near them.

Did you know that one of the pyramids of Egypt, called Sakkara, used to be sacred to a bird? The bird's name is the Ibis. The Arabs now believe that bird to be sacred, and a naturalist who visited Egypt said that if he or any other naturalist should take an egg or two from an ibis, or should kill a bird of that sort for scientific purposes, the Arabs believe that a curse would come as a punishment. In fact, when this naturalist did anything of that sort, his Arab servants used to call down curses on his head, and used to tell him that trouble would be sure to

overtake him. The naturalist said that he never abused his Arab servants in return, for he saw that they really believed what they said. Indeed, at last, the naturalist really became quite nervous about the superstition, in spite of himself.

The sacred Ibis used to be preserved by the Egyptians, and kept for hundreds of years after its death,

VIEW OF THE PYRAMIDS.

for the people thought that sometime the spirit of the bird would come back to its body. Of course that was a very foolish idea. But, as I think, people have a great many odd notions about birds.

Another bird that some English folks believe a queer thing about, is a relative of mine, the Raven.

THE SACRED IBIS.

You know that there is half-supposed to have been, hundreds of years ago, an English king named Arthur, and many interesting old legends are told about him. Well, some of the people who live in Corn-wall, England, think that King Arthur is still alive in the form of a raven, and some of the superstitious people will not shoot such birds, for fear of killing the king. All of this is nonsense, of course. The souls of people who die never come back to this world as birds. Still it is very helpful to us birds to have some notion abroad that will keep people from kill-ing us. I wish boys would believe something that would keep them from killing blue-jays.

Neighbor Pigeon told me a story about his folks, the other day. He says that a pigeon was used

once in deceiving people. A man named Mohammed,
wished to make the Arabs believe that he was a prophet
and received
messages from
Heaven. So Mo-
hammed taught
a pigeon to pick
seeds out of his
ear, and when
ignorant people
saw the bird do-

THE BERNICLE-GOOSE.

ing this, they thought that it was telling Mohammed
some news from Heaven. I think it was wicked in
Mohammed to cheat people so, don't you? But Neighbor Pigeon says that he does not think his relative
was to blame for eating the seeds out of the man's ear.

I hear queer things sometimes from Neighbor
Goose of the next yard. She was out walking yes-
terday, and she told me a thing that used to be
believed about the Bernicle-goose. She said that it
used to be thought that that bird came from a barnacle, a little shell-like being that lives on the rocks by

the sea. One kind of barnacle now has a name that means "the five-plated goose-bearer." An old writer named Gerarde, tells how it was thought that the goose came out of the shell of the barnacle. He said: "When it is perfectly formed the shell gapeth open, and the first thing that appeareth is the aforesaid lace

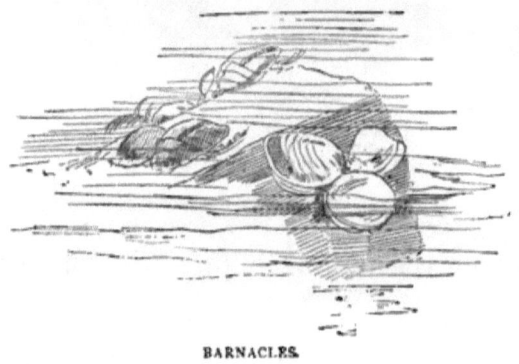

or string; next come the legs of the bird hanging out, and as it groweth greater, it openeth the shell by degrees, till at length it

BARNACLES.

is all come forth and hangeth only by the bill: in short space after, it cometh to full maturitie, and falleth into the sea, where it gathereth feathers, and groweth to a fowle."

Neighbor Goose was quite exasperated at such a story, for of course the geese all come from eggs, and not from such sea-things as barnacles; and Neighbor Goose says she should like to see any gosling growing

" to be a fowle " by falling into the sea after hanging
a while by the bill.

Neighbor Goose told me another queer thing, too,
and that was about the salaries of ministers in England, long ago. She
said that sometimes an
addition used to be
made to the salary by
allowing the minister to
have what was called
"goose-grass;" that is,

Royal Swan Mark.

he was given the right to let his geese run on the
Common.

Neighbor Goose said, too, that another relative of
hers, the swan, was thought once to be a royal bird in
England, and no subject could own a swan excepting
such persons as had received a " swan-mark."

The king used to have a swan-herd who looked
after the swans on the river Thames, and in other
parts of England, and if any one were found stealing
swans' eggs, he was punished by being put in prison,
sometimes for a year.

Neighbor Swallow, who comes past here occasionally, says that long ago there was a bishop in Norway
whose name was Pontoppidan — which was a dreadful
name, I think — and Pontoppidan said that some fishermen told him that they often drew up great bunches
of swallows from the bottom of the lakes, where
the birds had hidden during the winter. Whether the
Bishop Pontoppidan believed what the fishermen told
him or not, I do not know, but, any way, after that
notion was started by him a great many people did
believe it. And the story spread so widely, that at
last, in Germany, a reward was offered to any one who
would bring a swallow that had really been found
under water. The reward was to be an amount of
silver equal in weight to the bird brought, but no one
ever appeared to claim the silver. And no wonder!
Swallows did not winter in mud then, any more than
they do now.

But people have not been contented with telling
untrue things about real birds. There was an old
story about a bird that never lived at all. This bird's
name was the "phœnix." A man who lived long ago,

and whose name was Herodotus, wrote about this bird. He said that he had seen a picture of it, and that the people of Egypt told him that that bird visited them once in five hundred years. The picture of the bird made it look like an eagle with yellow and red feathers; and the story was, that there was only one phœnix at a time, and when that bird became five hundred years old, it built itself a nest out of twigs of cassia and frankincense, and in this the phœnix died. But from its body there came a worm that turned into another phœnix, that took the body of the old one and flew with it to the city of Heliopolis, where the body was burned. Some people said that the phœnix lived on air for five hundred years, and was then burned to ashes, and from these the new phœnix arose. Altogether, I think it was a very queer story, and I do not believe it at all. Do you?

I am going to tell you one thing more, and then I must stop. I heard it the other day, and it is only another proof to me that people did not know very much about us birds in the past, as I believe is the case now. There is in Europe a small bird, a kind of woodpecker, that is called the "wry-neck," because it moves its head continually. This bird is easily tamed, and boys sometimes tie a string to its leg and let the bird climb over trees. The bird eats ants and caterpillars, and has had a sad history on account of that habit of twisting the head all the time; for people in old days, seeing such actions, used to believe that the bird had some magic power. So the folks would take the poor wry-neck and tie it to a wheel with four spokes, which would be whirled around rapidly while certain charms were chanted. Wouldn't I have squawked, if I had been treated that way! Why couldn't the people let the poor "wry-neck" bob its head in peace?

A NUMBER OF HOMELY PEOPLE.

HOTINUS SUBOCELLATUS.

I AM a stranger to you, but please do not be afraid of me. I am a Chinaman — that is, I mean I have my home in China. My name is queer, too. It is Hotinus Subocellatus, and wouldn't it take you a long time to remember such a name, even if it were your own?

But besides my funny shape and my queer name, there is another very strange thing about me. I can shine at night in the dark. Once a man was in Hong Kong, China, and he saw some boys throwing stones at something on a wall. The something shone, and the man put up his cane and hooked the shining thing

down.   Then he took it into the house, and he found
that it was a Hotinus, just like me.

Well, I suppose that you think I am very homely,
so I will tell you about another homely person.
There is a very strange insect that lives in Brazil.
Shouldn't you think it queer if you saw a little bit of
an insect, about the size of one of the common house
flies, but with a sort of belfry above itself, and four
round knobs on the belfry, looking like the little bells
that people used to fasten on hawks?   And besides

Bell bearer

the bells there is a
sort of spike standing
out straight, as if it
were the bell-rope in-
viting you to ring.
The four " bells " are
covered with long
black hairs. The
" belfry " is not a part
of the head, but of the thorax, or the middle portion
of the body.

Another Brazilian insect has its thorax raised up

in two horns and lengthened out so that it covers the whole upper part of the body.

There is another very strange insect that has its thorax fixed in somewhat the same way, only instead of making a belfry and bells, it ends in two prongs that. look like a pair of sugar-tongs. This insect lives in the Philippine Islands, and I should think people might call it the "sugar-tongs bearer."

Hemiptycha punctata

But there is an insect in Mexico that looks more queer than most others, I think. It is green, and wears a little crest of yellow hair on its head, and on the under part of its body is a mass of white down. A man who once saw this insect, said that it looked as though some one had made it in a hurry out of cotton-wool. Besides the cotton beneath the body, there are long fibers that trail after the insect, and look as if they were made of cotton, too. If I were in that insect's place I should be afraid that those trailing pieces of cotton would be caught on something, but perhaps if they did, the cotton would break easily enough, so that it would not hinder the insect much. The insect's name is *Phenax auricoma;* and its latter name means "golden-haired," on account of the creature's yellow crest.

Hypsauchenia

A SEA-ANEMONE'S SIGHINGS.

SMOOTH ANEMONE (CLOSED).

I AM a captive, but I was not always one. In my youth I lived on the rocks by the sea. Many a charming little puddle was left there by the tide, and the live things in the puddle did taste so good!

I cannot tell you how many sand-hoppers I had eaten before the day when I was made prisoner. I do not get any sand-hoppers nowadays. My jailer gives me pieces of meat to eat, instead.

If I had known that any person was coming to take me away from my rock, I should have held on very tightly with my sucking-base, and resisted as much as possible. But, you see, instead of slipping

his thumb under me and gradually making me let go
of the rock, the man who is now my jailer took a hammer and hit a piece of the rock that I was sitting on,
and before I knew what had happened, that part of the
rock broke off, and I tumbled with it into the man's
basket. I was not at all hurt, though. That is the
best way to get us anemones If people try to pull us
off the rocks we are almost sure to be injured so we
do not live as long as people want us to. They should
take a hammer, if they expect to take us off whole.

The man took me home, and put me into a big
bottle where some seaweed had been soaking in sea-
water for an hour or two, and was all covered with
little bubbles of air. I was glad to find that such pre-
parations had been made for my comfort. I have
heard of poor sea-anemones being put into soap-suds
and living quite a while, too. But I am sure that
they could not have enjoyed it.

And I heard a shocking story the other day about
some anemones being put into a kind of liquor
called porter. An Englishman had brought the anemones to town with him, and one evening he and a

friend of his were looking at them. But supper-time came, and after the meal was over, as the things were being cleared away, the servant asked what should be done with the sea-anemones, and was told to put them into a jug.

Now the servant was a stupid, ignorant person, and there was only one jug on the table. This jug contained some porter, and the servant, taking the poor anemones, threw them into that jug.

The gentleman who had brought the anemones did not notice what the servant had done, and nothing more was thought about the poor creatures for two weeks, when the gentleman wanted to see them, and called for the anemone-jug. To his surprise, the porter-jug was brought, and there were the poor anemones alive, after their long soaking in liquor. Those are the only live anemones that I ever heard of that had anything to do with liquor of any kind. We are all temperance folks, but we do like to have our water salt.

Two other anemones were put into this bottle at the same time that I was. There are more than three

of us now, however. There are a good many little
anemones over on that pebble. Cunning little pink
things they are, too, and they spread out their wee
tentacles, and try to get food just as we older ones do.

Did you ever see an anemone fishing for food?

Smooth Anemone

(Fishing.)

We look very differ-
ently then from the
way we do when we
are shut up and rest-
ing. We will eat flies
if we can get them.
I heard of a man who
gave an anemone a
fly, one of the big,
blue-bottle kind. The anemone was very glad to get
it. Three or four days afterward, the man saw the
same fly floating on the water, and took it out, or
tried to do so, but the fly fell to pieces, for it was really
only the outside husk. The anemone had disposed
of the rest.

When my jailer gives me a piece of meat, I snatch
hold of it with my tentacles and draw it into my mouth.

Then I put the meat inside of myself. That is, I tuck
in all my tentacles, and the upper part of my body, too,
till I reach my stomach. Then I digest that bit of
meat. My arms are in my stomach, too, at the time,
but that does not trouble me at all. I know better
than to try to digest my arms. When I am through
with the bit of meat, I toss it out into the water. All
the nourishment has been taken out of the meat, and
only some white, stringy stuff is left.

Do you want to know what those jelly-like things
are that are scattered over this bottle? They are my
overcoats. That is, some of them are mine, and some
belong to the other anemones. You see, when I have
been staying in one spot for some time, and want to
move away, I throw off my overcoat and leave it behind,
to mark the place where I have been sitting. Not that
I care anything about marking the place, but throwing
off our overcoats is a fashion we anemones have. The
overcoat is a kind of jelly-like membrane that covers a
sea-anemone entirely, and sometimes it is very hard
work to pull it off. I was trying to strip one of mine
off the other day, and I really do not believe I could

have succeeded if that man who is my jailer had not helped me. He saw what I was trying to do, and he took a little camel's-hair brush, and reached down and helped me. It was very kind in him, and the minute I managed to pull that overcoat off, I spread right out and looked just as pretty as possible. He likes to see me look that way. Sometimes he holds me up to the light, and then he can see the sucking-base by which I move. I look very pretty then, for the dark-green lines that spread out from the center of my base show, and there is a row of blue globules around my edge among my spread tentacles. I suppose the contrast is very fine. The man says I am pretty, and I am glad if I suit him, for he is really very good to me.

There is a different kind of anemone down on the beach, a kind this man has not found yet. I think he will find it some day, though, he hunts the beach so diligently. The anemone's name is Bunodes, and instead of having a sucking-base of only one lobe, this anemone has a base of six or seven, so that Bunodes can attach himself to several separate stones and crevices. This makes it hard for any collector to capture

Bunodes without injuring him so that he will die. If the lobes of the sucking-base are injured at all, Bunodes is very likely to die.

SEA-ANEMONE.

But you ought to see that kind of anemone eat. He is a dreadfully hungry creature, and I tell you the crabs and the limpets have to be smart to escape from Bunodes. You see, he has a number of things called " thread-capsules " scattered over his body, but his tentacles are crowded with them, and when he wants to catch a

BUNODES CRASSICORNIS.

crab, he throws these little threads at him, and holds him until he is killed. Bunodes is quite powerful, for you know it is not an easy thing to hold a crab that wants to get away. But if Bunodes lays hold of even one leg of a crab the poor fellow must stay and be eaten.

I used to become acquainted with queer things down by the water. There were the red star-fish.

Uraster Rubens.

Sometimes children would pick them up and carry them away and come back to throw them into the water again, thinking they were dead. But the star-fishes often appear dead when they are not.

I used to meet a remnant of a Vilella sometimes. Did you ever see one? It looks as if it had hoisted a sail to the wind, but it is really a number of polyps living together and sailing the sea in company. The polyp that sits in the center is the one that eats for the company. I am sure that we anemones would never agree to form an association and let one of us do the eating for all. But it is dif-

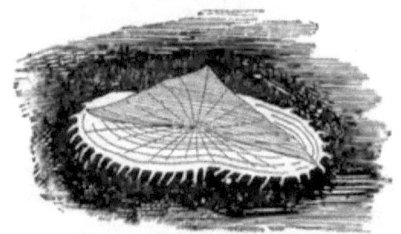

VILELLA LIMBOSA.

ferent with the Vilella folks. This central polyp does the eating, as I said, and a man who examined such

IN SEARCH OF STAR-FISH.

creatures, always found in the interior fragments of
shells and some remains of small fishes, showing what
the eating polyp likes for dinner. This polyp, since it
does all the eating, has to nourish all the other polyps
on board the Vilella.

Once a lady was walking on the seashore near me.
She had been looking at a dead Vilella, and then she
had picked up a star-fish, and she told a boy who was
with her that she had read that there used to be an
old law in the Admiralty Court of England, saying
that all those persons who did not treat star-fish badly
should be severely punished. The law spoke of those
who "do not tread under their feet, or throw upon the
shore, a fish called a five-finger, resembling a spur-
rowel, because that the fish gets into the oyster when
they gape open, and suck them out."

I am afraid that star-fish do attack small mollusks,
clams and mussels, but then, what are the star-fish
to do? Must they go hungry, with so good a dinner within reach? No star-fish is going to do that.
Some seamen call star-fish "five-fingered Jack."

Star-fish are very careful of their eggs. A star-fish

will gather the eggs together, bending its arms down-
ward, and arching its body so as to brood over the
eggs, the way a hen does, and if by any accident the
star-fish's eggs become scattered, the creature will take
great pains to gather them together again. The experiment has been tried in an aquarium, and it has
been found that a star-fish will travel the whole length
of its tank till the eggs are found and recovered.

That lady walked along a few steps past me, and,
stooping, she lifted a stone beside a pool. Something
whisked its winding length out of sight.

"Oh!" cried the lady, dropping the stone. "Why,
that was an eel."

" Let me have him," called the boy, running to the
spot.

But the boy could not catch the eel, try as he
might.

Both people sat down on the sand then, and the
lady told the boy something about eels. I do not
remember it all, but she said that there was once a
Roman called Lucius Crassus, who used to bring up
a kind of eel almost by hand. The kind of eel was

known as the muræna, and the ones Crassus had were so tame that they would spring out of the water whenever he came near them. Crassus would put on them rings and other ornaments, and one writer said that the loss of these eels was a greater grief to Crassus than the death of his three children. Crassus must have been a queer man, if that is true.

Some folks used to believe that eels grew from a kind of dew that fell in the months of May or June, on the banks of some particular ponds or rivers, and that in a few days by the sun's heat was turned into eels. In England, the fen-country called the Isle of Ely was said to be so named because of the great number of eels that lived there.

Some of the other things that came by when I was down by the sea, were the crabs. They crawled everywhere. Some of them were the little hermit crabs that carried shells around with them and changed shells occasionally. There were bigger crabs that walked around without shells, and one of them said that he was glad he had not lived in the days when some people used to practice " crabbing the parson."

I asked him what he meant, and he told me that there was once an old English custom of throwing

COMMON MADREPORE.

crabs in a shower on the "parson," or minister, as he went to, or came from, the chapel at the wake called "Kenelm's Wake" or "Crab Wake." People used to pelt each other with crabs for fun, I suppose, but if the crabs were alive they could not have thought it was very funny, for they must have been hurt. I believe "Crab Wake" came some time in July.

I forgot to tell you about the Madrepores. They belong to the polyps, and look somewhat like me. But how tightly a Madrepore will stick to a rock! You need to have a sharp knife if you are going to take off a Madrepore. The creature almost forms part of the rock itself.

Madrepores have little tentacles that look a good deal like mine. I have heard of a Madrepore that a naturalist once kept for several months. He could not coax it to eat anything but the least bits of meat. Feeding that Madrepore must not have been so easy as feeding me, I think, for the creature would not have anything to do with a small fly.

The Madrepore seemed healthy, and the naturalist said that he thought that its death was caused by a bad-tempered Daisy Anemone. The man usually stirred the water every day, so as to imitate as far as he could the natural stir of the sea, and one day when he did this the Madrepore was washed into the cave where the Daisy Anemone lived. And though the Madrepore was speedily put back in the little place of its own, a spot chiseled for it in the rock, yet the Madrepore never seemed to recover. It lived for a week or two, and then died, and all the naturalist had left was the Madrepore's skeleton.

I am sorry if the Daisy Anemone was so bad-tempered, but we anemones are not always kind to other beings, I must confess. Don't act as we do.

There was a queer creature called a sea-mouse that used to live in the mud by the sea. That sea-mouse was perfectly beautiful. Its bristles shone with wonderful color. That is, they would have shone, but the sea-mouse preferred to have its home in the mud, and of course light is necessary to show the beauty of the hairs, or bristles, that edge the body. The colors

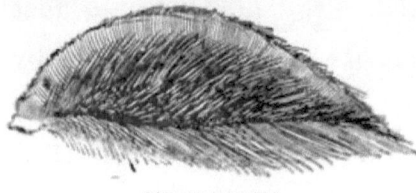

THE SEA-MOUSE.

have changing tints that flash along the bristles when they are moved. Red, white, blue, orange, scarlet, are colors that mark those bristles. A naturalist once said that it is certainly not possible to think of any structure more beautiful than these bristles.

And yet the sea-mouse hides in the mud. I believe that I have heard that pretty folks generally, among you human beings, like to be seen, but the sea-mouse is not very vain. If it is kept in an aquarium, the sea-mouse will usually stay in places so hidden by the weeds and stones that the owner will have to hunt to find the creature.

But these bristles are not only pretty, they are useful. The sea-mouse is thought to use them for defense, as a hedgehog uses its spines. The sea-mouse can draw in its bristles, though. If a hedge-hog should do that, I suppose the spines would prick him very much, instead of hurting other people. How do you suppose the bristles are kept from hurting the sea-mouse itself?

There is a very wonderful arrangement. Each little bristle has a double covering or sheath, and this closes when the bristle is drawn into the sea-mouse's body, and opens again when the bristle

Shell of Sea hare.

Shell of
Aplysia inia

comes out. The same naturalist who spoke about the beauty of the bristles said that it was hardly possible to think of anything in the animal kingdom more wonderful than these bristles. Indeed, I am very sure that no man could have thought of anything so beautiful and wonderful as a sea-mouse.

But if you should find a sea-mouse you might be disappointed at first, for its back is slimy because the discolored water has been strained through a great many fine hairs. The gills with which the sea-mouse breathes are underneath the back, and the water containing the air is filtered through the felt-like covering.

There is another creature called the "sea-hare" that has had strange things told about it. People used to look at sea-hares with horror in old times, and the fishermen of the Mediterranean Sea have so great a horror of the sea-hare that they cannot be bribed

Aplysia inca

to touch it willingly, and there are strange stories that are told by the fishermen of people's having had wounds, or mortified limbs, or having been killed by touching such creatures as these.

In old times in Rome, people said that the sea-hare was used to poison persons, and when a man named Apuleius was accused of magic, because he had married a rich widow, the greatest charge against him was that he had hired fishermen to get the sea-hare for him. Apuleius proved that what he wanted the sea-hare for was to satisfy scientific curiosity. But in those days, any one who hunted for the sea-hare was looked at with suspicion.

The poison that was prepared for the Emperor Nero was said to have had some sea-hare in it, and the Emperor Domitian was accused of giving the sea-hare to his brother. So, you see, there are some black stories connected with the sea-hare, and yet I do not think that he is so bad a fellow, after all. He is quite gentle and fat, and wears his shell inside of himself instead of outside.

A naturalist said that he had handled the sea-hare without having any unpleasant feeling from it. But another naturalist found at St. Jago a kind of sea-hare that has a sort of secretion spread over its body, and causing, he said, a sharp, stinging feeling. Another man said that as often as he took a sea-hare from the sea-water vase and put the creature on a plate, the room was filled with such an odor that his wife and brother had to go away. He could hardly endure it himself, and his hands and cheeks would swell after he had handled a sea-hare any length of time. So I think that the sea-hare cannot be good company for some folks.

A TREE-TOAD'S CHIRPINGS.

I DO not think that I have a very good time. An old German found me in the yard, and he keeps me shut up in a tall bottle. There is a little wooden ladder in the bottle, and you know that when it is going to be fine weather we little green German tree-toads like to climb. I go up that ladder at such times, but I stay down toward the bottom of the bottle when rainy weather is near. That German keeps me on purpose to tell him when to go to picnics. He looks at me every time he is invited to a picnic. If I am at the top of the bottle, he goes; but if I am at the bottom, he stays at home. So, you see, I am really quite useful to him. But I do not like being shut up in a bottle. I wonder if the tree-toads in other places are ever treated in this way.

But I am sure I do not have as bad a time as tree-frogs do in Australia. There are a great many of my relatives in that country. They are called Golden Tree-frogs, and whenever the natives have not enough food, they go out with torches at night and catch my relatives for supper. I have heard the German talk about it. He is quite a learned man, and he reads and talks about toads often, when he is near me.

I heard him say that I have some pretty relatives in Central America. They are not green like me, but they are sky-blue above and pink beneath.

The German read a good deal about the toad-stone this morning. You know people used to think that a toad had a precious stone in its head. The German read about the way the Italians said one could get this stone.

"Take a toad of those which have a red head," said the Italian, "place him in a cage upon a piece of scarlet cloth, and, early in the morning, set it in the rays of the rising sun. The toad will look fixedly at the sun, and you must let him remain there three hours, when he will cast forth his stone."

People thought that a toad-stone would cure any one who had been poisoned. People really believed in toad-stones in old times, and if a person had a stone and did not quite know whether it was a toad-stone or not, there was said to be a way of finding out. The German read about it:

"You shall knowe whether the tode-stone be the ryght and perfect stone or not. Holde the stone before a tode, so that he may see it; and if it be a ryght and true stone, the tode will leape towarde it, and make as though he would snatch it. He envieth so much that man should have that stone."

Well, no one need have worried about whether he had a real toad-stone or not, for there is no such thing. I am sure there is no precious stone in my head, and although I am not one of the earth-toads, yet I am sure they do not carry any such things in their heads, either. People were quite mistaken about us.

They were mistaken about another thing, too, for the German said that some English folks used to believe that there was one kind of frog that had its mouth naturally shut up about the end of August, and

that the frog lived so all winter. The man who wrote
about it in old times said that though this might seem
strange to some, yet it was known to too many people
to be doubted.

I am afraid that that man was easily deceived.
How in the world would any kind of a frog live after
its mouth had been
shut up? How could
it eat insects? And
the same man wrote
that some frogs turn
to slime in the winter,
and that the next sum-
mer the slime comes
to life again. I am

KIND PAPA FROG TAKES CARE OF THE EGGS.

afraid that that man, whose name was Izaak Walton,
never raised tadpoles and saw them turn into frogs.

I heard the other day of a frog that has the largest
tadpoles for its size of any of the frogs. This frog
lives in Guiana, and is green, spotted with brown. It
is called the " Jakie."

I heard the other day, too, of a very good papa frog

that lives near Paris. He takes care of the little tad-poles before they come out of the eggs. When such a frog as that is going to do such a thing, he sticks the eggs all on his back and goes away and buries himself in the ground. By and by when he has staid buried so long that the eyes of the little tad-poles begin to show inside the eggs, Papa Frog comes out of his hole and goes to some still pool. He jumps into the water, and there he lives, till, pretty soon, the eggs begin to open and the baby tadpoles come out into the water. Then, when all are out, Papa Frog's troubles are over, and he can leave the children to grow up by themselves.

I learned not long ago that in Bombay, India, there had been found some " Frog Beds." I thought at first that they were beds for frogs to sleep in, but I find that I have been sadly mistaken. They are not beds at all, but places in the ground where frogs that long ago turned into stone have been found. I am disappointed, for I had hoped that in my old age, when I should become a decrepit tree-frog, I might perhaps be permitted to rest my weary bones in one of those

" Frog Beds." But, alas! my hopes are gone. I must stay in this bottle and act as a barometer for that German. My comfort is, though, that if I hear him talk and read about frogs and toads much longer, I shall become the most learned tree-toad that ever was seen.

I forgot to tell you that the German said that folks used to think it lucky to meet a frog or a toad, because they thought that after meeting such a creature they would get money. The German read this aloud the other evening:

" Some man hadde levyr to mete with a *froude* or a *frogge* in the way than with a knight or a squier, or with any man of religion, or of holy churche, for than they say and leve that they shal have gold. For sumtyme after the metyng of a frogge or a tode they have resceyved golde — wele I wote that they resseyve golde of men or of wymen, but nat of frogges ne of todes, but it be of the devel in lyknesse of a frogge or a tode — these labourers, delvers, and dykers, that moost mete with frogges and todes, been fulle pore comonly and but men paye them their hyre, they have lytel or naught."

A queer story, but not a true one, used to be told about a man called St. Regulus and the frogs of Senlis. The story said that this man, Bishop of Arles and Senlis, found that the croaking of the frogs greatly interrupted him when he was preaching, and so he made a covenant with the frogs that he would not drive them out if they would agree to croak only one at a time. I do not know whether the story went on to say that the frogs agreed to this or not. I suppose so, for there used to be a chapel of St. Regulus at Rully that was decorated with frogs, in reference to this story, which, of course, is a made-up one.

A SEAL'S SAYINGS.

THE IGLOO.

WHEN I was little, I lived in an igloo. Do you know what an igloo is? Well, I will tell you how my mother made it, and then perhaps you will be able to think how it looked.

You know that seals keep open breathing-places in the ice, and as the ice grows thicker and thicker in the cold winter, so the tunnel that leads up from the water at a breathing-place becomes longer and longer. My mother had a breathing-hole, and one day she climbed straight up the tunnel to the top of the ice that covered all the water.

I suppose that you think that when she arrived at
the top of the ice she was in the open air. But you
are mistaken. There was a great pile of snow all over
the ice, and my mother poked her head into the snow
and scraped away at it with her forepaws till she had

made a sort of house with a
round snow roof to it. This
snow house, or "igloo," was
much wider than the opening
into the tunnel. In fact, the
igloo was quite a good little
room with sides and top of
snow, and an ice floor with

THE SEA-LION.

a hole in it, so that ma could go back into the water
when she wanted to do so.

Well, in that pretty little igloo I had my home.
My ma liked such a house for me to live in, because
she felt that I would be safe in it from the bears and
the dogs that like to eat little seals. Ma took care of
me very nicely. She could easily slip down into the
water and come back again, for the weight of the ice
and snow kept the water up the tunnel almost to its

opening into our igloo. Don't you wish you had been with me and found out how a seal lives in an igloo?

Sometimes people have tamed some of us seals. Once some person on the Shetland Islands, near Scotland, tamed a seal and kept her around the island for six months. When this seal, that had the name of "Sealchie," heard her-

MA COULD SLIP OVER THE ICE.

self called from a distance, she would answer, even if she were in the sea, and would swim ashore and awkwardly waddle over the stones and grass till she came to the lodge of her owner. But one day, when Sealchie was in swimming, a snowstorm came on and some wild seals coaxed her to go away with them. So her tamer lost her.

Some of the California Indians have a rather queer story connected with seals and sea-lions. The coast people of Northern California tell the story about a

great bed of mussel-shells and bones of animals that
exists at Point St. George.　This bed, the Indians say,
was left there by seven people called Hohgates, who
came to the place in a boat and built themselves
houses above ground, the way white men do.　The
Hohgates, say the Indians, came to the place about
the time when the first natives came down the coast
from the North, and the Hohgates used to live on elk
and on the seals and sea-lions, the people killing the
seals with a kind of harpoon that was made of a knife
attached to a stick, and all fastened to the boat by a
long line.　The Hohgates brought in their boats a
great many mussels, too, from the rocks, and of course
there were a great many bones and shells left from all
this eating.

But one day the seven Hohgates were out at sea
in their boat, and they harpooned a great sea-lion that
dragged them on at a terrible rate of speed.　The sea-
lion rushed toward a great whirlpool called Chareck-
quin.　This whirlpool was toward the northwest, and
the poor ignorant Indians say that it is the place
where souls go, where they shiver forever in darkness

and cold. There is a bitterly cold northwest wind — the Charreck-rawek — that sweeps over the place.

Toward the whirlpool fled the distressed sea-lion, dragging the seven Hohgates in their boat. Nearer and nearer they came, when, just as the edge of the dreadful whirlpool was reached, a wonderful thing occurred. Snap! went the rope, and down into the whirlpool plunged the sea-lion. But he was alone, for mysteriously the Hohgates were caught up into the air. Round and round their boat swung, going up higher and higher. No man on earth ever saw the seven Hohgates again, but the Indians say that there are in heaven seven stars that all men know, and these are the seven Hohgates that never more appeared on earth.

I suppose by the seven stars that all men know, the Indians mean the Big Dipper, but I am sorry for them that they should think that souls have to shiver forever in darkness and cold in that great whirlpool.

AN EARTH-WORM'S REMARKS.

A LOWLY PERSON.

I AM a very lowly person. Ploughing is my occupation. At present I am living in the side of that little trench that runs from the wood-shed to the fence. A number of other earth-worms live near me.

I have no eyes, and am deaf. Once a naturalist kept some earth-worms, and tried experiments to see if they could hear, but the worms did not mind the squeaks of a whistle or the loudest tones of a bassoon, and when the man put the earth-worms on a table near a piano, and the instrument was sounded as loudly as possible, the worms did not move at all, as though they had heard anything.

But although we earth-worms are deaf, yet we can feel sounds, if we cannot hear them. When that naturalist put the pots of earth on the piano, so that the worms could feel the vibrations, and then struck the notes, the worms were greatly frightened and went into their holes in a hurry.

This naturalist used to give his worms pieces of raw and roasted meat, and fasten such pieces to the earth by long pins, and he said that night after night he saw the earth-worms tugging away at such pieces, trying to eat them.

He found out, too, that we worms will swallow very sharp things, for his earth-worms swallowed the thorns of roses, and some small pieces of glass. We can do it, for all of us that swallow earth have gizzards that are lined with very strong membranes, and have very powerful muscles around them. We find our gizzards very useful, and we often put into them a number of small stones to help grind the earth. That naturalist used to give his worms glass beads and pieces of brick and hard tiles, and the worms swallowed them.

I have some relations in India that make little towers of earth-castings. Have you not noticed that we earth-worms have little piles of dirt at the openings of our holes? Well, these relatives of mine make small towers at their doorways. In Italy some earth-worms do the same thing, the towers being from two to three inches high. Inside of the tower a hole runs up to the top, so that the earth-worm can climb his tower and look over, if he wants to do so. But what the earth-worm really goes upstairs for is to bring up more earth and make the tower taller.

Some of my foreign relatives are very large, for a man who was in Ceylon once saw an earth-worm about two feet long and half an inch thick. I should feel very small beside such a monster.

In cold countries we earth-worms want to make our burrows deep into the ground, and it is said that in Norway and Sweden my folks burrow down seven or eight feet under ground, and in North Germany a man found worms frozen a foot and a half below the surface.

Salt water kills us earth-worms. Vinegar we all

hate, and it will kill us. Once a man had some barrels
of spoiled vinegar upset on some land of his, and the
next morning the man was very much astonished to
see the number of dead earth-worms that lay on the
ground. He had had no idea that there were so many
earth-worms in that piece of land. I presume you
would be astonished if you knew how many of us
there are in this trench.

I told you that ploughing is my occupation, and that
is true. We earth-worms regularly upturn the land,
and I think we are very useful folks. Long before
men invented ploughs we were at work, and that naturalist whom I told you about, and whose name was
Mr. Darwin, said that he thought it might be doubted
whether there are many other animals that have
played so important a part in the history of the world
as the earth-worms have. Whether that is so or not,
I hope we have tried to do the work that the One who
made us put us here to do. We are very humble
creatures indeed, but there is no one in too humble a
place to do any good. This is true even among men,
I believe. I am sure that even the weakest human

being must be able to do more good than a little earth-worm like myself, and yet even I am good for something.

I meet various neighbors of mine once in a while as I come near the surface of the ground. There are some black, lively little beetles that I do not care to become very well acquainted with. They are called " sun-beetles " or Amara, and I know that one of these little beings, when in confinement, will sometimes take

a bite at an earth-worm. That is the reason why I do not want to meet such beetles.

LARVA OF ONE OF THE CARABIDÆ.

When the Amara beetles are scared they will sometimes pretend to be dead. They belong to the Carabidæ, or ground beetles, and sometimes I have met their children. They are long, brown and white, and not at all the shape of the beetles.

Occasionally I find little piles of slug-eggs an inch or so underground. They are quite small, and some-what sticky. Little white slugs about an eighth of an inch long will come from such eggs after a while.

There are some other beetles sometimes traveling around this yard, in the corners and under the bushes. The beetles come here to help get rid of decaying meat on old bones, or dead birds, or mice, or anything like them. Sexton beetles they call themselves, and I think they are as useful as I am. Cleaning up is as

necessary as ploughing, I am sure. The Sextons that I have seen are dark colored, but there are some Sextons that dress more cheerfully, I have heard. One kind is yellow and black, and another is green, blue and coppery bronze. French

Sexton Beetle

people call the Sextons " Shield Beetles," on account of their flat shape and the way part of the body projects above the head.

The children of the " Silphas," as the Sextons are called, are flat and black. They are quite lively, but they often do not have a very pleasant odor to them. Indeed the word " Silpha " means " an ill-smelling insect." One of the Silpha beetles has a black spot that looks a little like a cross, on the back near the head, and a naturalist once gave this kind of insect the name of the "Crusader Carrion Beetle," because in old times each Crusader who went to help recover the Holy Land wore a cross on his coat.

One of the Sextons told me that there are beetles

that dare to live in the water. He said he knew it is so, because one night there was a light in the yard and several beetles flew over from the brook near this place. The beetles declared that they lived in the water, and Neighbor Sexton believed them. But an earth-worm would find it uncomfortable living in water, I am sure. I like a damp place; but when it rains so hard that I think I am going to be drowned, I crawl up on a board. A great many earth-worms at such times crawl on sidewalks and are crushed by people who walk the streets. I am sure that must be as bad as being drowned.

A TUSSOCK-MOTH'S COMMUNICATIONS.

LARVA OF ORGYIA LEUCOSTIGMA.

My name is Orgyia Leucostigma. Maybe you do not think that is an easy name to pronounce. Perhaps it is harder than your own. Well, then, you may call me the "Tussock-Moth."

Only I am not a moth yet. I am a hairy caterpillar. I am queer-looking — more so. than most caterpillars, too. In the first place, I have a sort of hump on my back, like a camel, only my hump is made of hair growing in four bunches. Then some of the rest of my hair falls over my forehead, as a little girl's bangs might over hers, only I never stop to curl mine. But the queerest things about me, the things that you would notice first, perhaps, are three stiff, dark brushes of hair that stand away out from my body. There are two on my head, shooting out like horns, and then there is one standing out of my back.

I was on the side of the woodshed the other day. I had been taking a walk, and I was wondering if I had better spin a cocoon, when some one touched me, and took me down from my place. The some one was a little girl.

She put me in her hand, and patted me with one finger, and said, "Poo' 'ittle patter-pillar!" She was a very small girl, and I suppose that she did not know how to talk plainly, and say "caterpillar." But I excused her, because she was so very gentle with me. I was afraid she would shut me up tightly in her hand and squeeze me to death, but she did not act so at all.

She carried me into the house to show me to her mother, and that lady put me into a glass tumbler and gave me a whole big apple-leaf.

That made me very happy. If there is anything that I like it is an apple-leaf. Sometimes I have eaten the leaves of vegetables, for I am not so very particular.

So I gave up all idea of making a cocoon just then, and went to eating. I ate quite a hole in that leaf, and the little girl stood and watched me do it.

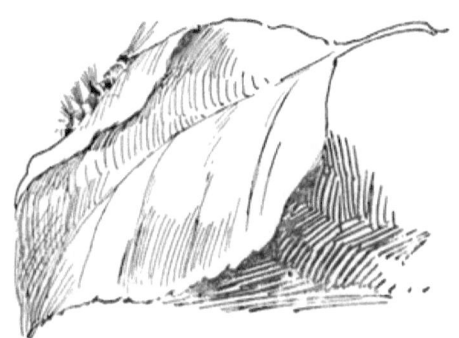

" SHE GAVE ME AN APPLE-LEAF."

Her mother told her that I shall turn into a moth. But I do not believe that her mother knows that although I shall be a moth yet perhaps I shall not have any wings. All moths do not have wings. Some of us Tussock Moths do not. My mother did not. I have heard so, at least, but I never saw my ma. She died when I was in a white egg.

This was my ma's life. She was a caterpillar; then she spun a cocoon and went to sleep; then one day she woke, came out, laid a number of eggs on top of the cocoon, and then died.

If I can fly when I come out of my cocoon I shall have pretty wings, and some feelers, or "antennæ,"

that look like very little toothed combs standing out from my head.

I think I am very fortunate in being a hairy caterpillar, because birds do not like to eat me, the way they do some kinds of smooth ·caterpillars. My hairy

COCOON OF TUSSOCK-MOTH.

covering has often protected me from danger.

Here comes that little girl with another apple-leaf. She brings me so many that I have hardly time to eat them. Every time she brings one she has to stop and pat me very softly. She says that I feel just like her "pussy-tat," and I should think that I might. But I do not think that I shall want to become very well acquainted with her pussy. Cats are enemies of moths and butterflies. I do not suppose that Pussy

would care very much about a hairy caterpillar like myself, but if I have wings hereafter I shall not come near her if I know it.

I wish I might fly high enough so that no cat could catch me. A butterfly that came by the other day told me about some big South American butterflies that are called Morphos. The largest of them sometimes measures seven and a half inches across the wings, and it is very difficult to catch such butterflies, because they fly so high. A man who had traveled in Brazil said that it was a grand sight to see the tremendous butterflies by twos and threes floating high overhead in the still morning air. The butterflies would flap their wings once in a while, but not often, for the man noticed the creatures sailing for a considerable distance without a stroke. One kind of the Morphos seldom comes nearer the ground than twenty feet, but its blue wings flash so in the sunlight that they can be seen a quarter of a mile away.

That little girl has an older brother who came and looked at me this morning. He was not very polite, for he said, "What a horrid caterpillar!" and then his

mother told him that he was like some men who used
to work in the same shop as a Scotch naturalist.

This naturalist was a poor man, and could not
always afford to spend his time on the hills collecting
insects, but in the summer he caught a number of
caterpillars, and used to bring them in a box and put
them beside him in the shop where he worked. Once
in a while some of these caterpillars would manage to
slip out of the box and go traveling around the room.
Some of the workmen did not care, but there was one
called Geordie, who was very much afraid of the caterpillars. He would become so terrified that he almost
went into convulsions when he knew that a caterpillar
was out of the box.

So the other men used to play tricks on Geordie.
They called a caterpillar a "lad," and whenever they
wanted to scare the man they would cry "Geordie,
there's a lad oot;" and then poor Geordie would jump
up and be very much frightened till he was sure that
every caterpillar was safe in the box.

The little girl's brother said that he did not think
that he disliked caterpillars as much as Geordie did,

and he did not think it was right in the men to say
there was a caterpillar out unless it was so. That
boy's mother has always taught him to tell the truth,
and I do not know whether the men that worked with
Geordie told the truth every time or not.

I am sure that no one need be so much afraid of
us caterpillars. It is silly to be terrified by a caterpillar, for it is only a moth
or a butterfly covered up in
a queer kind of dress, and I
am sure that folks are not
afraid of most butterflies or
moths.

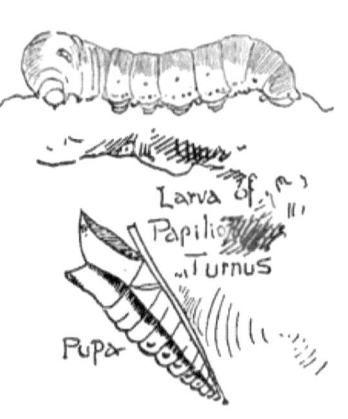

Some beautiful butter-
flies are going to let their
children feed this summer
on the apple-tree from which that little girl gets my
leaves. The butterflies are black and yellow, with
" swallow-tails," and are called Turnus butterflies.
Their children on the apple-tree will be little caterpillars that will be brown, spotted with black, at first.
Each caterpillar will have a large whitish spot in the

middle of his back. But when the caterpillars are
fully grown they will have changed their color and
become green. Then each caterpillar will turn into a
chrysalis, and if nothing happens a beautiful butterfly
will come out of each chrysalis. The Turnus caterpillars never have to wonder whether they will have
wings or not, for, if they live to be butterflies, they
are sure to have them. But I shall have to live on in
uncertainty for a while yet.

There is a queer caterpillar on that big thistle in
the yard. The caterpillar is so hidden that if you did
not know exactly where to look, you might not see
her. She lives alone; not in a company, the way
some caterpillars live. She is inside one of the thistle
leaves. I think it is about the tenth leaf from the top
of the thistle. She has drawn the two sides of the
leaf together so as to hide herself, and there she stays
and eats thistle. I should not think she would like
such food.

I heard her say once, that some day she should
turn into a chrysalis marked with gold spots, and after
that she should come out and be a " Painted Lady."

She said that is the name given to her beautiful kind of butterfly that has five spots on the under side of each of the hind wings. That kind of butterfly has another name, but it is so hard a one that the " Painted Lady " caterpillar had to say it over half a dozen times before I could remember it. It is " *Pyrameis cardui.*"

But I suppose that living on thistles is nothing.

Why, some butterfly caterpillars actually live on nettles, and seem to think nothing of it. There is a butterfly called the " Nettle Tortoise-shell " that puts its eggs on the under side of a nettle-leaf, and the caterpillars eat nettles as if they were good. The caterpillars of the " Peacock butterflies " in Europe eat nettles, too.

You need not think that the butterflies have all the pretty names, for there is a moth in Europe called the " Night Peacock." The caterpillar of this moth has a queer way of leaving one end of its large, pear-shaped cocoon open when making it, but nothing can come in to harm the creature, for the fibres of the co-coon are arranged so that while the moth, when it is ready, can go out easily, all other insects are kept out. Is it not wonder-ful that God should have taught a caterpillar how to weave the cocoon over itself in so protect-ing a way? I am sure, since he cares for us poor caterpillars, he must care a great deal more for boys and girls, they are so much bigger and more important than we are.

NETTLE TORTOISE-SHELL EGGS.

I think if that little girl's brother who thought I was "horrid" could see the caterpillar of the "Lobster moth" he would not think me the most ugly caterpil-lar that ever grew. The "Lobster moth" caterpillars are very queer. They live in forests on beech or oak

PEACOCK BUTTERFLY OF EUROPE.

or birch-trees, and are pale brown or leather color.
Oh! if you could see the queer shape and the two tails
of such a caterpillar you
would think you had found
a strange creature, indeed.

"NIGHT PEACOCK."

The English country
people know a creature that
they call the Puss Moth, and it has a caterpillar that
the French call the Fork Tail. The caterpillar has
two tails, like the Lobster Moth caterpillar, and it has

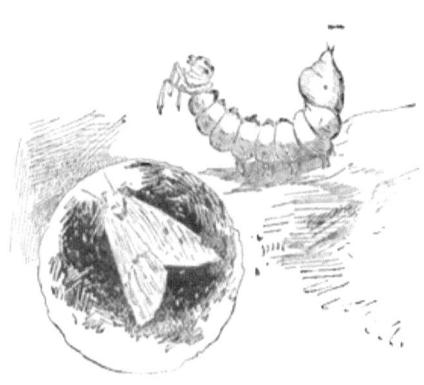

THE LOBSTER MOTH.

been thought possible
that the Puss caterpil-
lar uses them to scare
the dreadful ichneu-
mon-flies that are the
enemies of so many
caterpillars. But I
think this is only a
guess.

One of the geometric or "measuring worms," or
"drop-worms," as people call them, is a little like
me, because its moth sometimes has no wings. The

moth's name is the "Mottled Umber," and when it has
no wings it looks somewhat like a spider.

One of my near relations is Orgyia antiqua, which

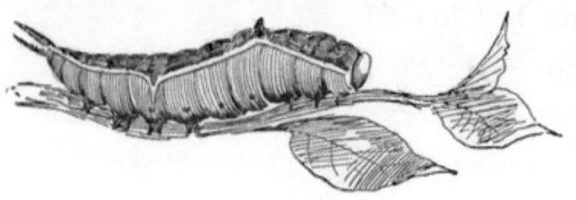

THE PUSS CATERPILLAR.

has a brown
moth, called
the "Vaporer
M o t h." I
myself shall
be brown-winged, if I have any wings, but there will
be a white spot near the outside of each of my wings,
and I shall be a darker brown than the Vaporer Moth.
There is another near relative of mine called Orgyia

pudibunda, and its caterpillar
has a queer name. It is the
"Hop-dog," though I do not
know why such a name should
be given to any member of
the caterpillar family.

THE PUSS MOTH.

Probably there is a reason for it. There is a
reason for almost everything, I find. One of the butterflies was saying only the other day that she had
discovered the reason for the name of the "Caliper

Butterfly." That is a quite rare butterfly that has been found in Java, I believe. A man once caught a

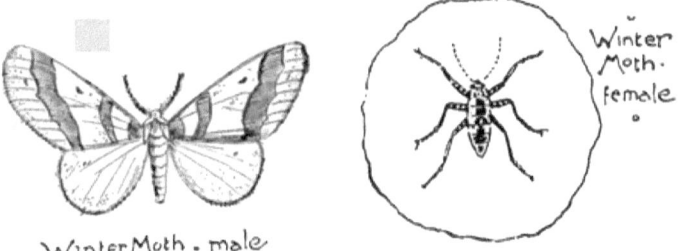

Winter Moth. female

WinterMoth - male

specimen as the butterfly was sitting sucking the liquid from a muddy spot by the roadside. The butterfly sat with its wings up while sucking. On each

CALIPER BUTTERFLY.

hind wing are two curved tails, and they look like a pair of calipers. Do you know what calipers are? They are compasses; not like those the little girl's brother uses in drawing at school, but compasses, with curved legs, meant for measuring the diameters of round bodies. That Caliper butterfly must have been disgusted to think it staid so long drinking that it was caught. The most easy way of taking the finest butterflies of warm countries is to draw near the butterflies when they are drinking.

The man never saw another butterfly like his Caliper one, and when he wrote about it he said it was still the only butterfly of its kind in English collections.

A PHOLAS' PROTESTATIONS.

Pholas
Dactylus

WELL, suppose I did squirt that sea-water into your face! It was good enough for you. What did you come along here with your hammer for, and split the rock I lived in, and take me out? I guess if I want to live in a rock all my days, I have a right to do so, and who are you with your hammer? I'll throw all the sea-water I please on you.

You're not going to eat me, are you? Pholades are good to eat. Oh! I didn't mean to tell you that. Don't eat me, please, will you? I'll tell you all I know about myself and my folks if you won't. I'll stop squirting water at you, too. I suppose I should have to stop soon, anyway, now that you have taken me out of my rock and away from the tide. You are sure that you are not going to eat me?

Well, then, let me collect my senses and see what

I can think of to tell you. You see it is exciting to be taken out of my hole — my hole that I expected to always live in. Just see how you and your hammer have spoiled it. My hole

I SEND THE PARTICLES UP ONE OF MY SIPHONS.

that I bored in that rock myself.

How do you suppose that I make a hole? I have a kind of rasp to bore with. The fore part of my shell is set with stony points in rows, and I bore away, turning from side to side, not clear around, but holding myself in place by my foot. My shell itself is made of a substance called aragonite, which is harder than the rock in which I bore, so that my shell will not be too quickly worn out. Isn't that good? If my shell

wore out you had better believe I would stop boring.
It would not feel very comfortable to have my body
rubbing against rock, I suppose. But we rock-crea-
tures, as well as others that do not live in rocks, are
wonderfully made, so that we are fitted for our sur-
roundings.

I rasp off the rock, as I said, but how do you suppose I get rid of the particles? There I am inside my
hole, and the particles might bother me, but I send
them up one of my siphons into the water. Part of
the rock-particles lodge between my valves and the
stone, forming a soft mud. A man once watched some
Pholades that were at work in a tide-pool in the chalk,
and he saw a cloud of chalk-powder come out once in
a while, and noticed a heap of such powder around the
mouth of each burrow.

You see, my "siphons," as they are called, are two
tubes that reach from me and my shell up the hole to
the water outside the rock. The two tubes are close
together, like a double-barreled gun, and through one
tube, or siphon, I draw in the water. This contains
the air that I must have for breathing. The water

passes over my gills, and then goes out up the other siphon. I send the rock-particles up, too, when I am boring, as I said.

In such holes we Pholades live and die, and you may find very good shells of dead creatures by splitting open rocks. Even compact limestone may be bored by us. It is very comfortable to sit at the bottom of a hole, and let your long, stout, yellow siphons run out and bring you in what may come. There is a kind of Pholas that is found in the English Channel and the Atlantic Ocean, and lives buried in the mud, or in decaying wood. Along the French coast Pholades are called "Dails," and are hunted for to be eaten on account of their fine flavor. Now, remember, you promised not to eat me.

But let me tell you one thing. You know that a great many mollusks shine in the dark. We Pholades do, and if any one were eating us raw in the dark he would look as if he swallowed phosphorus.

We are palatable enough, people say, so that it is not absolutely necessary to cook us. But I think I had better stop talking about this subject of eating.

Some way I keep mentioning it every few minutes, and that won't do. I am afraid you will become hungry, but I suppose you are a truthful person, and will keep your promise to me.

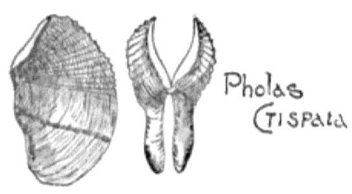

Pholas crispata

Are you going to let me go and bore another hole? I heard about a Pholas that once bored into something besides rock. A lady once was watching some Pholades that were in a basin of sea-water. They were boring, and the lady noticed that two of

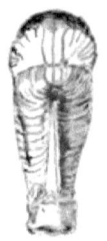 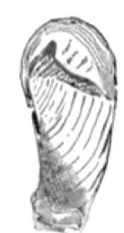

them were boring at such an angle that their tunnels would meet. She wondered what would happen then, so she kept on looking.

By and by the two tunnels

Pholas Melanourae did meet, but one of the Pholades was stronger than the other, and what did the strong one do but bore straight through the weaker one, as if it had been only a piece of chalk. Wasn't that terrible? I am sure I do not want any Pholas boring through me with that rasp. I think the lady must have been shocked at what she saw. What must she have thought of the manner of us Pholades?

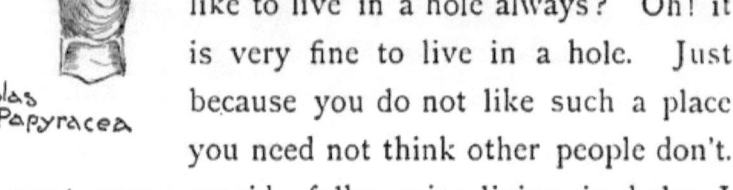

Pholas
Papyracea

You should not think that I would like to live in a hole always? Oh! it is very fine to live in a hole. Just because you do not like such a place you need not think other people don't. A great many seaside folks enjoy living in holes, I assure you. Only the holes are often made in the sand instead of in the rock.

There are my neighbors, the Razor-shells, in holes on the sandy beach. A Razor-shell will pass his whole life in a hole, sometimes going up to the top, and sometimes going down to the bottom of it. And

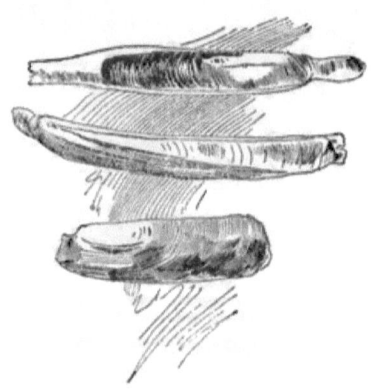

RAZOR-SHELL, OR SOLEN.

that is journey enough for a Razor-shell to make.

Sometimes a fisherman who wants to catch a

Razor-shell tries to do so, but the man has to be careful, for the Razor-shell is very quick. As the tide goes out, the fisherman walks along looking for the jet of sand and water that the Razor-shell throws out when frightened by the man's footsteps. If Neighbor Razorshell would not do that, I think likely the fisherman would not know where the hole is, but after that jet appears, the man plunges a narrow iron rod into the hole. The rod has a barbed head that may pierce the poor Razor-shell, and hold him till he is dragged out of his hole. But if the fisherman misses his aim the first time, he does not try again with the same Razorshell, for the man knows that the creature will have gone down to the bottom of the hole, and there is no getting him out of there.

Neighbor Cockle likes to dig his hole in the sand, too. He digs with his foot, which is a kind of natural spade. He can dig almost as fast as a man can with a real spade. But Neighbor Cockle does another thing with his spade. He uses it to jump with. I do not see, for my part, why he should want to jump, but he does. He stands on his foot and springs up into the air. I am sure that I behave in a more dignified manner than that, usually.

But, dignified or undignified, you human beings seem to eat us all. Ever so many of Neighbor Cockle's folks have been eaten, and a great many of mine, too. But you promised not to eat me, you know. Now will you let me go? If I must bore my-

Common Cockle.

self another hole, I had better be about it. Don't tell anybody where I make my hole, will you? I do not want any more visitors. One such visitor as you have been is quite enough for a lifetime. I trust I shall have no more callers to watch me while I am at work.

There go the wild ducks. Do you know, I believe they are going to call on the short Razor-shells, on the beach? The wild ducks are delighted when they find a number of those Razor-shells, and sometimes a man has seen what it is that interests the ducks, and has come shell-gathering, too. I had rather keep away from both ducks and men.

Good-by. I am going to bore as hard as I can. This rock is not so difficult to tunnel as the hard blue clay that my cousin, the Rough Piddock, bores into. There is another kind of Piddock in California that is economical, I think, for he makes use of the rocky dust that he gets from boring. What do you suppose he does with it? He builds a chimney. It's a fact. As though a rock-borer did not have enough to do without building, as well as boring! But this Piddock seems to think that his siphons are not sufficiently protected, and so he builds a strong, conical chimney for them. How wasteful he would think I am! Throwing away rock-dust! I am glad he is not here to tell me how economical his folks always are.

And if I tried to follow his example and build, a pretty chimney I should make. He would know how to do it without failing, and he might make fun of me. Oh! I am very glad that he is not here. I am going to throw all the rock-dust I get into this puddle of sea-water.

At least, if I am not economical, I am not so mean as another of my relatives. His name is Martesia, and he is quite small, but he is occasionally a nuisance. He will sometimes bore into a large shell while its owner is living, and may carry the burrow so nearly through the pearly shell-lining that the owner has to build up a round knob to protect himself. I hope I do not bother other folks as much as that.

"DADDY" AND HIS DIPTERA.

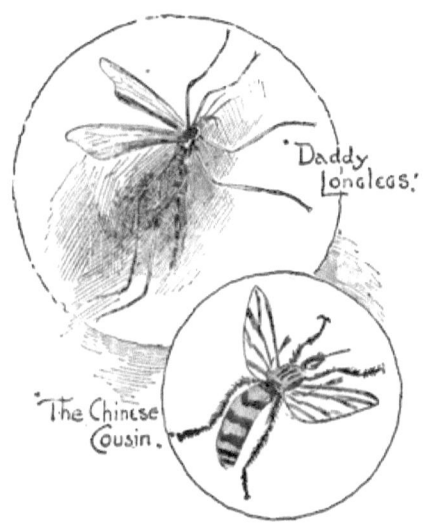

Daddy Longlegs.

The Chinese Cousin.

So you call me "Daddy Longlegs," do you? Well, I suppose my legs are quite long. But I have been so used to being called a "leather-jacket" that it seems queer to have any other name. However, I suppose that I must remember that I am no longer a grub in the ground, and that is the reason why my name is changed. When I was a grub I had no feet, and I was soft and round and of a grayish color. I lived on the tender roots of grass in the meadow. I do not think that the farmer liked me at all, for he did not admire any of my folks. But I should like to know why I had not as much right as he had to those grass roots. He used to grumble a good deal about us "leather-jackets." He called us that because of the leathery skins we wore.

He need not have grumbled so much, though. I should like to know what he would say if he had some other kinds of Diptera here. You know that we 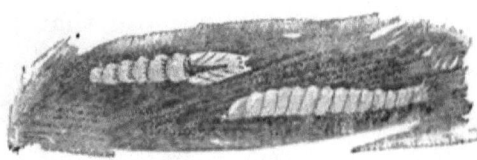 "Daddy Longlegs," and all kinds of flies, belong to the Diptera, because we have only two

LEATHER-JACKET.

wings, instead of four, like the butterflies.

Well, the members of the Diptera that I meant I should like to have the farmer see, are some flies that will even catch honey-bees, and kill them in spite of the stings. And that farmer has three hives of bees himself, and I think he would be angry enough if any such flies as those came around catching his bees. He would stop thinking about the "leather-jackets"

then. The flies that catch bees have some big, beautiful Chinese cousins that are bright yellow and black.

But there is another one of the Diptera that I think
the farmer would be even more angry with than the
bee-catcher, and that is the " Tsetse fly." Did you
ever hear about
him? He and
his folks live in
Africa, and they
are small — about
as large as com-
mon house flies —

and you would never think, to look at them, that they
are dangerous creatures. They live on river banks, but
they will often stay in swarms on one side of a river,
while on the other side there will not be a fly. This
Tsetse fly bites, and that is the reason why I think
the farmer would be angry. He has a cunning little
red calf that he thinks a great deal of, and if one of
those Tsetse flies should bite that calf it would die,
for the bite is poisonous to such creatures as horses
and cows, sheep and dogs. The fly bites persons, too,

but it does not harm them much, for the pain soon
goes away. While it lasts the feeling is a good deal
like that of a mosquito-bite.

But people who have cattle in Africa always dread
coming to any place where the Tsetse flies may be.
Of course people in such districts could not have pet

dogs, but folks can
keep goats and pigs
and mules, for the
bite of the Tsetse fly
does not kill them.

The native Afri-
cans pretend to have
roots that they can
pound and sprinkle

on the hair of cattle, and in this way prevent the
Tsetse fly from biting them. But this is all nonsense,
for the cattle of the Africans die just the same as the
cattle of other people. When the natives are obliged
to go with their cattle through a country where the
Tsetse fly is known to live, a moonlight night in
winter is chosen, so the Tsetse will be too cold to bite.

Another fly that might frighten that farmer by its appearance is one that lives on the Molucca Islands. This fly has so very long a beak that it looks like a sort of spear.

But there is one of the Diptera that I think the farmer ought to like, and that is a fly by the name of

SYRPHUS PYRASTIN.

Syrphus. There were several such flies around here to-day, and the reason why the farmer ought to like them is, that their larvæ eat the plant-lice, or Aphides, that attack his vegetables. The Syrphus fly puts an egg in the midst of a company of Aphides, and when that egg hatches there comes out of it a little green, or green-and-purple, worm without any eyes or legs. Of course such a worm could not travel far for its food, but it does not need to. It is in the midst of its food.

The worm has a queer sort of mouth, with a little three-pronged fork to it, and the worm catches an Aphis on this fork, and sucks the creature nearly dry. Then the worm catches another Aphis. By and by the worm has grown large enough, so it stops eating and sticks itself to a leaf; its body draws up and becomes hard, till it looks like a little bag. And it is from this bag that a Syrphus fly, spotted with gold and looking like a wasp, comes after a while.

A TALK BY AN ANT.

THE BAT'S FAVORITE POSITION.

I HAVE been to see a bat. He was a little fellow, about six inches across his wings. I found that bat before the cat did. I was walking along the path by the rockery, and I found that bat lying dead in the way. I do not know what had ailed him, but I went up and peeped into his almost shut mouth. Then I looked at a foot of his. It seemed like a human being's wrinkled hand with the fingers all the same length, and the finger-nails all allowed to grow long and kept whittled to points.

Maybe that boy over the fence killed the bat some way. I do not know. I was thinking of going and telling the rest of the ants in my hill about what I had found, when a cat and a woman and a little girl came along.

"Why, Pussy, what is that you have?" asked the woman.

She took up the bat.

"Why, it's a bat, isn't it?" she said. "I believe I will put him into some ants' nest, and let them skeletonize him, if they will. I'd like to keep the skeleton for my class. No, Pussy, you cannot have this bat. Why! here is an ant on it. Shoo!"

And she blew me off.

I fell to the ground. The woman drove the cat away, too. · She did not want the cat to know where the bat was to be buried.

I felt quite bewildered by my tumble, but I recovered my senses and started home. When I arrived there I found everything in confusion. That woman had chosen my ant-hill and dug into our nest and put the bat there. We ants would not have cared so

much for that, but she had dug out a great number of small white ant-pupæ, the children of our nest. I found a great many of our folks running around seizing the ant-children and rushing away as fast as possible to hide them. We were all dreadfully worried for fear the children should not be safely put away.

Ant Larva

The ant-children are in different stages of growth. In some of the pupæ the limbs and the head of the coming ant can be seen,

Ant. Pupa

under a microscope, but all pure white. Others show yet no limbs, and might easily be called "ant-eggs," as some people who do not know any better do call them. Of course the ant-children cannot run around yet. They are about three-thirty-seconds of an inch long, and their brownish eyes contrast plainly with their white bodies. One can see the numerous dots that compose each eye. There are fifty facets, or corneas, in the eye of an ant, though one kind of ant is said to have about a thousand.

I do not like it at all to have that woman dig into our ant-hill so. There might be some excuse for her if she believed what some folks thought once. There was a knight in old times who was known as Sir John Maundeville. He was quite a traveler, and he wrote a narrative of his travels; he wrote in this all the wild stories he pleased, and he told about an island called Taprobane where there were great hills of gold that the ants kept full diligently. If that woman believed in finding gold in ant-hills nowadays, I should not so much blame her for digging into our house.

But we ants have had a great deal said about us that is not so. There was an old Greek historian, Ctesias, that said that there were ants that were as large as foxes. I don't believe he ever saw any. And then I heard once what another man, Herodotus, said about ants. He was talking about a sandy desert somewhere, and said he: "In this desert, then, and in the sand, there are ants, in size somewhat less indeed than dogs, but larger than foxes. Some of them are in the possession of the king of the Persians, which were taken there. These ants, forming their habitations under ground, heap up the sand, as the ants in Greece do, and in the same manner; and they are very like them in shape. The sand that is heaped up is mixed with gold. The Indians, therefore, go to the desert to get this sand, each man having three camels.

"When the Indians arrive at the spot, having sacks with them, they fill these with the sand, and return with all possible expedition; for the ants, as the Persians say, immediately discovering them by the smell, pursue them, and they are equaled in swiftness by no other animal, so that if the Indians did not get the start of them while the ants are assembling, not a man of them could be saved."

There! What do you think of that story? Wouldn't you like to see an Indian, with three camels and some sacks, fleeing before a pack of ants "larger than foxes"? It seems to me that folks must have known very little about ants, to tell such a story as that.

People in old times used to have another queer idea. They thought that they could get a stone that would keep other folks from seeing them as they walked around.

"Take water," said an old writer, "and poure it upon an ant-hill, and looke immediately after, and you shall finde a stone of divers colours sente from the faerie. This beare in thy righte hande, and you shall goe invisible."

That woman who dug into our ant-hill has never tried this plan. I am sure I hope she never will. Perhaps she does not believe in any stone that will make her "goe invisible." Neither do I believe in it, and I hope she will not come pouring any water around here. It is bad enough to have to remedy the evil she has done now, digging into our house with her spoon, without having to be half-drowned, too. But she is right about one thing. We ants can clean small creatures so as to leave their skeletons in good shape. People can wire the bones together afterward.

She says she wants the bat's skeleton for her class, so I suppose she does not have any nonsensical idea such as was formerly told about the bones of a green frog that had been eaten by ants. It was said that if the bones of such a frog were taken, those on the left side would provoke hatred, and those on the right side would excite love.

I hope that cat will not discover where the bat is, and come here to dig it up. Last September when the winged ants were rising from their holes, the air in spots was alive with the creatures; that cat thought she would catch ants and eat them. Perhaps she did not think that the fluttering things were ants. Most of the ants she had seen did not have wings.

Well, she caught some, but I do not think that Tabby chewed more than two or three or so. She went and sat on a board, and I think she let the ants alone after that, although they were flying behind her. We are quite protected from danger sometimes by the way we taste. Very few insects like to eat us. Spiders do, though, sometimes.

ANOTHER VOICE FROM A MENAGERIE.

THE ARABIAN CAMEL.

Now, while that hyena was talking about the animals in this place, why in the world didn't he mention me? I am sure I am as worthy of being talked about as any of the other animals, and, if no one is going to talk about me, I shall talk about myself. I know I am not very pretty, but then, think of my stomachs!

Almost every one has heard about a camel's three stomachs and the water-cells in them, but all people cannot remember that in an Arabian camel like myself the cells will hold a whole gallon and a half of water. But sometimes it is very unfortunate for us to have such stomachs, for on long marches across the desert, the Arabs, when without water, will occasionally kill some camels to get at their cells.

But, beside our queer stomachs, our noses a r e made in a strange way. You know it is very un- pleasant indeed to have sand blow up your nose, but we

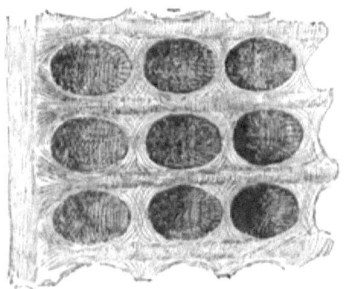

WATER-CELLS OF THE CAMEL'S STOMACHS.

camels are so made that when the sand-blasts come we can shut up our noses with some little valves in- side. Don't you think that the One who made us camels was very kind to fix our noses so that we should not be suffering all the time?

Our feet are made so they are just right, too, for we have very thick soles, so that the hot sand of the deserts cannot burn us. Altogether I think we camels ought to be very thankful that we are made so beautifully. Some of the old Jewish rabbis did not think we were very thankful though, for they had a saying, " The camel desired horns, and his ears were taken from him." I think, though, that the rabbis made up that saying to tell to people who were grumbling and who ought to have remembered how much worse off they would have been if the good they had were taken away from them. Most people are not nearly thankful enough for their good things. It is so much easier to grumble than to be thankful.

Do you see that little fellow over there that looks somewhat like me, only he has no hump? That is my South American cousin, the Llama. In their native country llamas are used for carrying loads of silver from the mines down the narrow trails of the mountains.

The llamas have Indian drivers who are often very kind to them. If a llama is tired and falls behind the others, or lies down, the Indian driver will go back and talk to it and try to make it forget how tired it is. Sometimes, however, the llamas, when very much hurried, become angry and spit at the Indians. Some people say that such spittle is poisonous, but I do not believe that is true. Any way, Cousin Llama over there has never poisoned any one since he has been here.

A man was looking at me the other day, and he said that a bigger camel than I am had been found in Hindostan. Unfortunately I shall never see that camel, for long ago he turned to stone, and he is now a "fossil," as that man called him.

THE LLAMA.

That hyena that talked so much did not tell you all that I know about his folks. I suspect that he was ashamed to have you know how greedy his relatives are. This is the thing I know: Once, when a great traveler named Livingstone was in Africa, he was much troubled by a large number of hyenas that came near his camp and laughed very loudly for two whole nights. Livingstone knew that the natives he had with him thought that hyenas had some intelligence, and so he said to the men, "What are the hyenas laughing at?"

And the men answered that they thought the hyenas were laughing because they knew that Livingstone and his company could not eat all the provisions and plenty would be left for the hyenas to eat.

But, whatever they laughed at, I am sure that Livingstone must have wished that they would keep still nights and let him go to sleep.

But there is no politeness about a hyena. In fact I do not very much like any of those animals in that row of cages yonder. I cannot see what makes them scream, and lash their tails, and yell, and rush from one side of their cages to another, every time that keeper goes by with the meat-cart. Meat does not look so very good to me.

It is a fine thing that those beasts are shut up. I am afraid that if one of them were out he might attack me. There is that cage holding the cruel Wolf, next to the Coyote-cage. I have watched that wolf enough to know that the old Greeks and Romans were wrong. You know that hundreds of years ago, when my great-grandfathers were traveling the deserts, the Greeks had a belief that if a man and a wolf met, and the wolf saw the man before the man saw him, the man would become dumb. And so the Greeks had a saying, " To see a wolf," which meant, "to be struck dumb." Well, I have watched people going by that wolf's cage, and even if they did not look at the wolf and he did look at them, yet the folks went straight on talking and never became dumb at all.

Maybe most of the folks who go by that cage never think of it, but, about a thousand years ago, the people over in England were so much troubled by wolves that the Saxon king, Edgar, said that every criminal who would kill a certain number of wolves should go free, and the Welsh people saved themselves from having to pay a tax of gold and silver, by killing three hundred wolves, instead.

It was high time that something of the sort should have been done in England then, for in the reign of a king who ruled a little time before Edgar, and whose name was Athelstane, the wolves were so numerous that a refuge had to be built in Yorkshire for such travelers as were attacked by the animals. The old Saxon name for January used to be " Wolf-moneth," because the wolves were hungry and troublesome in the winter. I am glad that those wolves are killed now, and I should not object to seeing that old fellow in that cage killed, too.

Next to the Wolf-cage is the Tiger-cage, you see. Neighbor Tiger is a treacherous fellow. He says that the people of India are very much afraid of his folks, so much afraid as to hardly be willing to mention the word " Tiger." The people usually speak of him either as " the beast," or else will not name him at all.

Next is the Monkey-cage, and I rather like the creatures in there. I have heard that some of the people of Borneo, the Dyaks, think that their long-nosed monkeys used to be men. The Dyaks say that the men did not like to pay taxes, and so they took to the woods and became monkeys. But you need not believe this story.

I think that monkeys do look a little like folks, and I know that when some missionaries went to Africa they found that the people all along part of the west coast believed that the gorillas were real people.

The Hindoos, in India, have a great many monkeys that are called sacred by the people. The creatures are Hoonuman monkeys, and they have black hands and feet. The Hindoos say that the way the sacred monkeys came to have black hands and feet was this :—

THE MANGO.

Long years ago, there was a good Hoonuman monkey that noticed that the people of India did not have the fruit called the mango. Did you ever see a mango? It is red or yellow outside, and soft and juicy inside. Well, this kind-hearted monkey determined that the Hindoos should have some of this fruit and be able to raise it themselves. So the monkey went on a journey over to the island of Ceylon.

In that island there was a garden owned by a giant, and the monkey went into this garden and stole some mangos and carried them back to the Hindoos.

But the monkey was not satisfied. Although he had been kind to the Hindoos, yet he hated the people of Ceylon, and he determined that he would burn them up. He took a lighted tar-barrel, and was going to set fire to the whole island of Ceylon, but some way the barrel was tied to the monkey's tail, and instead of hurting the island at all he only succeeded in burning his own hands and feet so badly that they turned black, which was good enough for him, I think. If a person will try to injure other people, something bad almost always comes to him himself. But the Hindoos say this is the reason why their holy monkeys have black hands and feet.

I am sure that this story is not true, and I should think that the Hindoos would be ashamed to tell about their sacred monkeys being so wicked as to try to burn up people.

The people of India say that it is very unlucky for a person to build his house on the spot where a

Hoonuman monkey has been killed, and if a person does build there he will die. So, out of respect to this nonsense, whenever the natives build houses some one of the wise men has to be called upon to tell by his wisdom whether a monkey's bones are to be found on the spot where the house is to be built; and if the wise man says that a sacred monkey has once died there, then the house must be built somewhere else. And so afraid of bad luck are those people that not one of them will ever acknowledge having seen a dead monkey.

The people of the island of Ceylon have sacred monkeys, too, and the people pretend to believe that the body of a dead monkey of that kind has never been found in the forests. And there is a proverb among those people, " He who has seen a white crow, the nest of the piddy bird, a straight cocoanut-tree, or a dead monkey, is certain to live forever."

Do you know that monkeys hate snakes ? Once a naturalist, Mr. Darwin, took a stuffed snake and carried it to a place where a number of monkeys were kept. They were greatly excited, and gathered around staring at the snake. In the cage was a little wooden ball with which the monkeys had often played, but they became so nervous from looking at the snake that, when the ball happened to roll a little, away rushed all the monkeys greatly frightened.

Another time the same man put a live snake into a paper bag, and, closing the top of the bag, put it down where the monkeys could go to it. After a little while, one of the monkeys saw the bag, and came to find out what was in it. As soon as the monkey had seen what was there he rushed away, but, in spite of the supposed danger, the other monkeys could not endure it not to come and peep at their enemy in the bag. Monkey after monkey came and peeped at the horrifying sight.

I once heard, too, of a baboon that could be made very angry by his keeper's taking a letter and reading it to him. I do not know why it should have made the baboon so angry, but Mr. Darwin saw this monkey once when he was being read to, and the baboon became so angry that he bit his own leg until the blood flowed from it.

Baboons were thought a great deal of in the Middle Ages, and were brought over to Europe from Africa and sold. No gentleman was thought to be in fashion who did not own an ape. The apes were dressed and taught to be polite, and sometimes they were allowed to come to feasts with the fine folks. There used to be a queer old story told about an ape and the mischief he did once when he was dressed like a man. I do not think that the story is true, though. It would be a sad thing to have a man killed on account of an ape's actions. The tale is named this way, "Of the Welcheman that delyvered the letter to the Ape."

The story is that once a man was arrested for some crime. Now this man had been a servant of a gentleman, and when the gentleman heard what the trouble was, he wrote a letter to the chief justice asking him to let the servant go free. The gentleman gave this letter to a Welshman, and told him to carry it to the chief justice and bring an answer back.

The old story says, " This Welcheman came to the chefe justyce place, and at the gate saw an Ape syttynge there in a cote made for hym, as they used to apparell Apes for disporte. This Welcheman dyd of his cappe, and made cortyse to the Ape, and said, ‘My master recommendeth him to the lord your father, and sendyth him here a letter.’

“This Ape toke this letter and opened it, and lokyd upon the man, makynge many mockes and moyes as the propertyes of Apes is to do.

“This Welcheman, because he understood him not, came agayne to his master, accordynge to his commandes, and told hym he delyvered the letter unto the lorde chief justice sonne, who was at the gate in a furred cote.

“Anone hys master asked hym what answer he brought.

“The man sayd that he gave him an answer, but it was French or Laten, for he understode him not. ‘But, syr,’ quote he, ‘ye need not to fere, for I saw in his countenance so muche that I warrent you he wyll do your errand to my lorde his father.’

“This gentleman in truste thereof made not any further suite, for lacke thereof his servant that had done the felonye, within a month after, was rayned at the king's bench and corte, and afterwards hanged."

There is one kind of South American monkey called the Capuchin, that has its face ornamented with a beard. The Capuchin is a very strong, fierce monkey, and it is very hard to tame him. One of the things that he is the most particular about is his beard. He cannot bear to get it wet, and so when he drinks, instead of putting his mouth down to a stream, he takes up some water in his hand, lays his head over one side on his shoulder, and drinks out of his hand very slowly and carefully so as not to wet his beard. A traveler once said that if a person wanted to put this kind of a monkey into the greatest possible rage, all he would have to do would be to throw some water on the Capuchin's beard. The person who did that would find out that such an act is an unpardonable sin in the monkey's sight.

You see, I hear a great deal in this menagerie. There is a kind of bear that I should like to see. He is not in this menagerie. His name is the "Spectacled Bear." He is called that because although the

greater part of his face is black, yet around his eyes
he has two light-colored rings that make him look
exactly as if he were wearing a pair of goggles.
Those who have seen him say that he is very funny-
looking.

Indians tell queer stories about bears, sometimes.

The Rukh—after
a Persian drawing.

The Euroc Indians
in Northern Cali-
fornia are afraid of
forest-demons that
are supposed to live
in the forests and
take the form of
bears that shoot
arrows at travelers
that are out by night. But of course that is not a
true story at all. There are no such things as forest-
demons, and I should have thought that the Indians
would have found that out, long ago. Some of the
California Indians used to burn their dead to prevent
them from turning into grizzly bears. It is sad to
think what foolish ideas the Indians have about such

things. Some of the Indians near Trinity River used to believe in a sort of spirit called Omahá that had the shape of a grizzly bear. He could not be seen, but the Indians believed that he went about everywhere bringing sickness and trouble to men.

There were two other enemies that those Indians believed in. One was named Makalay, that moved with great leaps like a kangaroo and had a horn like a unicorn. If any human being saw Makalay the sight was thought to bring death. I do not

RUKH'S EGG.

think many people could have died from that cause. How could they when there was no Makalay to see?

Then there was a third dreadful creature, called Kalicknateck, that the Indians thought was a great bird that sat on top of a mountain and when hungry would sweep down over the ocean, catch up a great whale, carry it to the mountain, and then eat the whole whale for a single meal.

That reminds me of a story I once heard of another bird that the fables of old times called the Rukh. A traveler named Marco Polo told of the bird, and people said that the sound of its flying was like loud thunder, and the bird was so strong that it would seize an elephant in its claws and carry him high into the air.

It seems to me that, if people really believed in that Rukh, they must have dreaded seeing any such creature come swooping from the sky. But I can hardly think that many persons would believe very sincerely in such a bird.

A SHREW'S STATEMENTS.

MY NOSE IS TOO POINTED FOR A MOUSE.

Now, little boy, you are mistaken. I don't care if I do look like a mouse, I am not one. My nose is too pointed for that; don't you see?

I am a Shrew; no relative at all of the mice. My relatives are the Moles and the Hedgehogs; that is, we are all classed under the "insect-eaters," and we sleep in the daytime and go out at night to hunt food. We shrews live under rubbish, or in holes in the ground. Some of us like the water very well.

People used to dislike us because they thought we did mischief. The Italians had an idea that the bite of a shrew was poisonous, and the Roman people used to call a shrew *mus araneus*, or a "spider-mouse," because they thought that a shrew threw poison into its bite, like a spider.

French and English people disliked us, too, because they thought that we made horses and cattle paralyzed, and some of the ignorant folks even went so far as to say that, if a shrew ran over an animal's foot, the animal felt great pain. So, when a horse, or cow, or sheep, that had been out in the fields, was found to have a numbness in its limbs, the people would say that it was "shrew-struck."

And this idea brought much trouble to us poor shrews, for the cure for an animal that was "shrew-struck" was thought to be a switching with a branch of a "shrew-ash," as it was called. Now a shrew-ash was made in this way. An ash-tree was chosen, and with an auger a hole was bored deep into the tree's trunk. Next, a poor shrew was caught and put alive into the hole, and then the hole was plugged, and the unfortunate shrew was left to die of hunger. This cruel act was supposed to give power to the ash-tree

to cure " shrew-struck " cattle, and whenever afterward
a horse or a cow was supposed to be troubled in this
way, a person would go to the "shrew-ash," pull off
one of its branches and gently switch the animal with
it. This was said
to immediately
take away all pain
from the animal.

But I feel very
sorry that so silly
an idea should
have caused any of
my relatives to be
starved to death.

THE WATER SHREW.

That is worse than being killed by a cat, because a cat
does kill one after a little time, but it must take a
good while to starve to death. I never liked cats,
though, and I am ·surprised to see how many people
prefer them to us shrews. Why, I heard the other
day of a man who spent a good part of his time
making pictures of cats. His name was Gottfried
Mind, and he lived in Switzerland quite a while ago.

But although he made so many pictures of cats, they were all different, and they were so natural that they really looked as if they were alive, and I think a shrew that was bright enough to notice a picture would not have liked those Gottfried made.

He painted the pictures of so many cats and kittens that he was called the " Raphael of Cats," and travelers came to see him and get some of his cat-pictures.

But, one year, a thing occurred that was very dreadful, according to Gottfried's ideas. Some of the people of the town of Berne became frightened about some signs of madness that had shown itself among the cats, and so, for fear that the creatures should really go mad and bite people, the magistrates of Berne gave orders that the pussies should be killed.

That was an alarming order to poor Gottfried. He had a pet cat named Minette, and he managed to hide her, but alas! eight hundred other cats were put to death.

Gottfried was dreadfully shocked, and it is said that he never became wholly comforted. But, after the killing-time was over, he went to work harder than ever making pictures of cats, and the next winter he went into the business of cutting chestnuts into the shape of cats. He made chestnut-cats that looked so cunning that people bought them as fast as he could make them.

GOTTFRIED MIND'S FAVORITE.

But I have never heard of a painter who cared very much about making pictures of shrews. I do not see why, either, for I am sure we are very cunning. We are not very pretty when we are babies, though, for then we are blind and without fur. If a painter wanted to keep shrews for models he would have to have a separate cage for each one, for I am sorry to say we are quarrelsome, and kill one another when shut up together.

I have heard that not only painters have liked cats, but musicians have done so, too. It seems strange that our enemies should be so honored and we neglected. For instance, I heard a story the other day about a cat that made a piece of music. I do not mean that the cat made it all, but she only started it. There was a musician named Dominico Scarlatti, who had a favorite cat that used to sit on his shoulder while he was playing. And so fond was this cat of being patted that as soon as Scarlatti stopped playing the cat would jump down on the keys of the instrument and try to attract the musician's attention.

One day some of Scarlatti's scholars were talking together about a kind of musical composition called a "fugue," and one of the scholars said that he thought it was very hard to find anything for the basis of such music.

Just then Scarlatti's cat jumped on the keys, and the cat's paws struck five notes. The musician said that he did not agree with the scholar at all, and to prove to him how easy it is to take any notes for a foundation for such music, Scarlatti took just the five

notes that his cat had struck and made a piece of
music out of them. That piece of music is called
"The Cat's Fugue." I have heard, too, of another
musician who composed some music called "The
Bees' Wedding," but I have not yet heard of any one
who has made any musical composition regarding
shrews. I do not think we have been appreciated and
honored as we ought to have been.

Tunicate.

A MAN was walking by this shore a while ago. He was a very learned man, but he was much astonished at something that he had found among the sea-weed. The something was pink, about the shape of a pear, only very much smaller, perhaps as large as two strawberries might be.

The man held the something in his hand. The thing seemed to be spongy when he felt of it.

Just then a boy came along.

"What kind of a fruit do you call that?" asked the learned man, holding up the thing he had found.

The boy looked at it.

"Oh! that's a piece of sea-pork," said he carelessly.

"Sea-pork!" repeated the learned man, looking astonished, "what is that? I never heard of it before."

"I don't know," answered the boy. "It's alive; that is, some pieces are. But folks around here just call it sea-pork."

Now I could have told that learned man all about "sea-pork," for I am one of those live creatures myself. Our name is "Tunicates," because we are covered by a kind of leathery tunic or coat. Some people call us "Ascidians," which is a very good name to describe us by, for it comes from an old Greek word that means "a skin bottle."

We do look like some queer sea-fruit. Some of us are six inches long, others only one inch.

Long, long ago there was a man who has been called the "Father of Zoölogy." His name was Aristotle, and he tried to find out whether we Tunicates should be called animals or only vegetables. You know that when we are fully grown we have a stem that fixes us to rocks or mud and that makes us look like some queer vegetable growing.

Aristotle was a sharp old fellow, and he knew how to use his eyes. So he looked at us, and at last he said that we were animals and not vegetables. And he spoke the truth.

And this is what he wrote about the covering we Tunicates wear: "It may be cut like dry leather. They have two separate openings which are very small and difficult to notice, one to take in and the other to eject the water."

Now, when I was little, I was a kind of tadpole. That is to say, I had a tail, and by means of wriggling it considerably fast I swam through the salt water. I had, too, some things that looked like arms.

But after awhile I fixed myself to a rock, and my tail vanished. I sent out projections that looked like roots, two holes appeared in me, and I began to look like a full-grown Ascidian, or "sea-squirt," as some people call us, because when we are touched we squirt out water.

I am sorry to say that a man who tried to study us Ascidians became blind from looking at too small things. You see, some of us Ascidians are compound;

that is, a great many little ones live close together inside of the same skin, and this man, whose name was Jules Savigny, and who was the first man of modern times to find out what we Tunicates are, strained his eyes too much by looking at things so little as one of these mites of Tunicates would be. So that great naturalist lost his sight, and I am sure he must have wished that he had not tried quite so hard to study " sea-pork."

When a great many of us live together inside of one skin, each of us sometimes has his own heart and breathing system. In other kinds, the separate Tunicates become mixed under the skin.

Sometimes, when you have been to the seashore maybe you have turned over big stones and have found under them jelly masses of different colors — yellow, green, blue, or purple — with stars on them. Those were my relatives, Tunicates. I have in Greenland a different relative that has a covering that is not leathery like mine, but horny, and is called Chelysoma; from two words that mean " a tortoise " and " body."

But I have some other relatives that I do not believe you have ever seen. They are called *Pyrosoma,*

or "fire-body," because they shine. A man named
Mr. Huxley once wrote about these shining relatives
of mine. He said that it was hard to catch them as
they floated in the sea, because they were not on the
surface, but deeper down. But some were caught and
put into a bucket. The creatures did not shine all

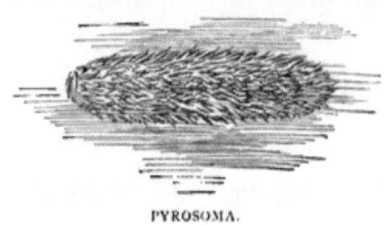

PYROSOMA.

of the time, but the light
would sometimes be quite
bright, and then in a few
seconds it would begin to
fade till all was dark.

Another man saw
some of these shining relatives of mine when he was
at sea in a squall. There were great multitudes of
the creatures floating on the waves, and he said that
those Tunicates near the surface of the water looked
exactly like small, shining cylinders of iron.

I myself can neither swim nor shine, but I know
that those Pyrosoma folks are from two to fourteen
inches long, and I think that a fourteen-inches one
must be quite a sight when it makes up its mind to
shine. I should have said their mind, though, for

one of those cylinders is made of ever so many small creatures placed side by side.

I have some very tiny red relatives that float freely, too. Once, when some men were cruising off the north coast of Scotland, they saw cloudy red patches of coloring matter in the water. Some of the red matter was dipped up and put under a microscope, and the red turned out to be some of my little relatives. These relatives are said to be the lowest form of us Ascidians, and they have a name longer than themselves, I think. The name is Appendicularia.

We Ascidians cannot see, and we have no shells, of course. We have hearts, though, and our blood circulates; but there is one queer thing about us. Sometimes our blood will turn back and flow in the opposite direction from that in which the current has been going. In those Ascidians that live all together, each has its own heart and breathing apparatus, but the circulation of the blood is common to some extent.

One of the Ascidians is red and about the size of a currant, and in some places this relative of mine usually lodges in oysters. This troublesome person has a near relative that is a parasite on living lobsters.

I forgot to tell you one thing about my Pyrosoma relatives. A Brazilian named Bibra once caught six Pyrosoma, and, as he was on ship-board, he used them to light his cabin. The light given out by the Pyro-

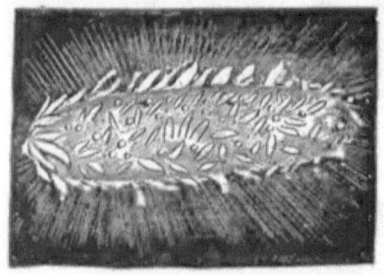

"ANIMAL LIFE."

soma was bright enough so that he could read to one of his friends a description he had written of the little light-bearers.

A naturalist once sailed on the warm Mozambique current east of the cape. He afterwards told what he saw. He said that quite suddenly as they entered the warm current the ocean seemed full of life. The whole sea was covered with animals of various kinds, and for more than two days the folks sailed through fields of giant Pyrosomata that "swam so close together that at night the whole ocean, out to the farthest horizon, shone with their blue gleam as if in broad moonlight."

BOSSY'S MOOINGS.

IT is too bad that Mrs. Cutkeedahcut has such afflictions. She is a very troubled hen, and all her sorrow has been caused by the white cat. He is a rascal, and I believe he has eaten all of Mrs. Cutkeedahcut's chickens this year. At least, I saw him eating Chippy, the youngest of Mrs. Cutkeedahcut's infants, and her others disappeared mysteriously.

I take great interest in all the inhabitants of this barnyard and I am sorry for Mrs. Cutkeedahcut, notwithstanding her unkind remarks about the intellect of cows. She always was a gossiping hen, but the time that she made fun of cows was once when she was very tired of sitting on the eggs before the chicks came. Maybe her being tired made her feel more like making impolite remarks, but any way she began to

cackle about the stupidity of cows in general, and she
told a story about a cow in the southern part of Asia;
Thibet was the country she mentioned, I believe.

Well, Mrs. Cutkeedahcut's story was this: It seems
that two men were traveling in that country, and one
day a Lama herdsman who lived in the same house
with them came, looking very sad, to say that a little
calf of his was dying.   Now the cows in that country
are very hard to milk, and the herdsmen almost always
let them have their calves near at milking-time, so that
the cows will lick them and will not pay much attention
to what the milkman is doing.

But how was the Lama to milk his cow, now that
the little calf was dead?

This was what Mrs. Cutkeedahcut said that Lama
did.   He took the skin off the little dead calf and
stuffed the skin with hay.

The next morning, when milking-time came, the
herdsman took the milk-pail in one hand and the hay-
calf under the other arm and started for the cow-yard.
The hay-calf had neither head nor feet, for the Lama
had not thought it necessary to add them.   He laid

the hay-calf down before the cow. She looked at it, smelt of it, and believed that it was her own little calf. So she began to lick it, and the man milked peacefully.

And that cow, so Mrs. Cutkeedahcut said, really continued to believe that that was her calf. At last, one day, in the midst of her licking, some place in the calf-hide broke, and the hay that the calf was stuffed with came out.

Then, Mrs. Cutkeedahcut said, almost any one would have expected that the cow would have seen through the cheat, and would have been angry at the way she had been deceived.

But that cow was not. She did not seem to be in the least surprised, but began to eat the hay! And Mrs. Cutkeedahcut said that she believed that cows think that calves are stuffed with hay, usually.

I do not know whether they are or not, I am sure. I don't see any reason why they might not be. I have seen them eat hay.

Mrs. Cutkeedahcut said that she should like to see any person stuff a dead chicken with hay and give it to her for a real one! She did not believe that any one could do that and cheat her.

But I know one thing, Mrs. Cutkeedahcut is not

so very smart, for once she sat on a porcelain make-believe egg for three weeks, and expected to have a chicken from such a thing. So hens are not so very much more smart than cows, after all.

I told Mrs. Cutkeedahcut that any way calves used to be worshiped in old times in Egypt.

MRS. CUTKEEDAHCUT.

And then Mrs. Cutkeedahcut said that was wicked.

But just then the rooster reminded her that hens used to be thought sacred in old times by the Druids in England.

I told her that she ought to be ashamed to have

any connection with the old Druids. And so the remarks went on.

But I am really sorry for Mrs. Cutkeedahcut in spite of her evil remarks, for all her five children are gone, and nobody has brought her back even a stuffed hay-chicken for her comfort.

I was glad while they were talking of so many old-time things that one fact that I am ashamed of was not mentioned. Perhaps the folks in this barnyard never heard of the fact, and I need not have felt worried lest any one should speak of it. Sometimes, when the old Highlanders wanted to know anything about the future, they would take the hide of a cow and go off to some lonely place. There one of the men would put on the cow's hide, covering all of himself but his head. Then he would wait in the darkness and fog till he thought that some invisible beings had given him answers to the questions he asked. What the cow's hide had to do with so silly a practice I do not know, but the Highlanders were very superstitious.

I suppose that Mrs. Cutkeedahcut would be

pleased to learn that a Scottish chief once lost his
right of chieftainship for speaking of killing some
hens. This young chief of Clanrannald had just
returned to take possession of his estate, and, when he
noticed how many cattle the people had killed in honor

SITTING ON A MAKE-BELIEVE EGG.

of his coming, he very
foolishly said that if
they had killed a few
hens it would have
done just as well as to
have wasted so many
cattle.

The clansmen were
very angry at this re-
mark, for they thought

it showed that the young man did not care much for
the feelings of his people, and they cried out, "We
will have nothing to do with a hen-chief," and they
immediately took the chieftaincy from the young man
and gave it to one of his brothers. But I suppose if
I should tell this story to Mrs. Cutkeedahcut she
would indignantly inquire why a "hen-chief" was not

as good as a "cattle-chief," so I suppose I had better keep still about the matter.

From this barnyard I can see a peach-tree over the fence where the orchard begins, and that tree sometimes makes me think of a foolish thing that used to be said about cattle. It was that if the leaves of a peach-tree fell before their time, that was a sign that cattle would be sick or die. But I do not find that the growing or falling of the leaves of that peach-tree affects my health in the least.

www.ingramcontent.com/pod-product-compliance
Lightning Source LLC
Chambersburg PA
CBHW031110020726
47495CB00007B/2138